AN IMPETUOUS PROPOSAL

"Taking an unwanted bride seems an awful price to pay for securing your lands," Felicity said. "Tell me, is it worth it?"

Kilgarvan looked at her in amazement. "You would not understand."

"How can I, unless you give me a chance?"

He looked at her steadily. "Kilgarvan is the most beautiful place in the world. Nowhere else are the valleys as green, the lakes and rivers as clear, the people as warm and welcoming. There is nothing I would rather be than the FitzDesmond of Kilgarvan. I would do anything to save its people . . . even take an English bride."

The fierce passion in his voice stirred something in Felicity. In that moment she envied him with every fiber of her being. She would gladly trade every pound of her inheritance for the certainty that Kilgarvan possessed. Here was a man who knew who he was and where he belonged.

She had not known what she wanted until she heard him speak. And now she knew that what she wanted more than anything on earth was to share his sense of belonging.

"Marry me," she said without thinking.

BOOK YOUR PLACE ON OUR WEBSITE AND MAKE THE READING CONNECTION!

We've created a customized website just for our very special readers, where you can get the inside scoop on everything that's going on with Zebra, Pinnacle and Kensington books.

When you come online, you'll have the exciting opportunity to:

- View covers of upcoming books
- Read sample chapters
- Learn about our future publishing schedule (listed by publication month *and author*)
- Find out when your favorite authors will be visiting a city near you
- Search for and order backlist books from our online catalog
- Check out author bios and background information
- Send e-mail to your favorite authors
- Meet the Kensington staff online
- Join us in weekly chats with authors, readers and other guests
- Get writing guidelines
- AND MUCH MORE!

**Visit our website at
http://www.zebrabooks.com**

THE IRISH EARL

Patricia Bray

Zebra Books
Kensington Publishing Corp.
http://www.zebrabooks.com

ZEBRA BOOKS are published by

Kensington Publishing Corp.
850 Third Avenue
New York, NY 10022

First Printing: March, 2000
10 9 8 7 6 5 4 3 2 1

Printed in the United States of America

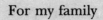

For my family

Author's Note

Although I drew my inspiration for this story from my travels in Cork and Kerry, the town of Glenmore is fictional, as are the family of FitzDesmond and the Earl of Kilgarvan.

One

Lady Felicity Winterbourne stood on the steps of the New Theater, pausing to adjust her cloak, wrapping it tightly around herself to ward off the chill night air. The crowd swirled around her and her escort, but she took no notice of them.

"Was not the performance marvelous? I daresay this Farnsworth will soon rival Kean in his fame. I can't think of when I have seen a finer play," Sir Percy Lambeth exclaimed.

Lady Felicity glanced at her escort. "I will grant you that John Farnsworth was adequate as Hamlet," she said. "But the actress who played Ophelia was far too old to be convincing, and forgot half her lines. And the ghost was drunk and missed one of his entrances."

Her tone was sharper than she had intended, and her escort winced. "Of course, of course," Sir Percy said, nodding his head vigorously to indicate his agreement. "It is as you say."

Lady Felicity bit back a sigh. She had chosen Sir Percy Lambeth as her escort this evening because of his affability. Sir Percy's chief talent was in making himself agreeable to all. He would pronounce even the most deadly dull of events to be delightful. The least mark of favor or condescension was cause for lengthy exclamations.

He had declared himself delighted and honored when she had first allowed him to escort her, and since then had shown himself to be her devoted servant, agreeing eagerly with every word that she uttered. It was enough to drive her mad. At first she had suspected hypocrisy. But now she knew better. Sir Percy had no opinions of his own. He lived only to please others, and measured himself by their opinions of his worth.

Before meeting Sir Percy she had been convinced that a gentleman who strove to make himself agreeable would be the best sort of husband. But as her acquaintance with Sir Percy improved, she found herself questioning her convictions. Perhaps there was such a thing as being too willing to please.

Sir Percy looked up toward the portico where his mother and sister stood waiting, and then down at the street below, which was thronged with vehicles of every description. But apparently he did not see the one he was looking for. "My coachman is late," he fretted. "But my carriage should be here presently."

Around them the theatergoers swirled, descending the steps toward their own vehicles. The steps of the New Theater and the courtyard in front were filled with society ladies and gentlemen, rubbing shoulders with those from the pits. Orange sellers and women of dubious virtue hovered at the fringes of the crowd, advertising their wares. There were the hubbub of voices, the creak of carriages and the cries of coachmen.

Above the din she heard a voice calling. "Please, my lady, can you spare a coin for a crippled soldier? My lord? A penny for a hot meal?"

A one-armed man, dressed in tattered rags, slowly

made his way through the crowd at the bottom of the stairs. He repeated his beseeching cry, but not one of those present would meet his eyes.

Lady Felicity felt something stir inside her. These days beggars were a common sight in London. One could hardly walk a block without hearing the cries of the unfortunate. Soldiers left idle after the victory over Napoleon, laborers who had been displaced by the new factories, even whole families of tenant farmers who had lost their land as a result of the Corn Laws. She could not help them all, and yet . . .

The one-armed man repeated his call, shuffling listlessly along the edge of the crowd. But he might as well have been invisible, for all the attention he received.

She reached in her cloak pocket for her purse, but her hand found only empty space. She bit back angry words. As a lady she was not expected to carry a purse, especially in the evening. That was for servants or gentlemen.

"Sir Percy, lend me a crown," she said impatiently.

He goggled at her. "Whatever for?"

"I don't have time to waste with questions."

Sir Percy began unbuttoning his cloak.

She began making her way down the stairs, certain that Sir Percy would follow. But before she had taken more than a few steps, she saw the beggar pause as a gentleman approached and called to him.

The gentleman spoke to the former soldier. She continued down the stairs, but could not hear what they said. Then the strange gentleman reached inside his cloak and withdrew his purse. She could not see what he gave the beggar, but it was clear that it was more than a single coin that he pressed into the beggar's remaining hand.

The former soldier's face was transformed, apathy replaced with desperate hope, as if he were a man dying of thirst in the desert who was afraid to believe that he had found his long-sought oasis.

The gentleman gave a parting admonition, then turned to leave. His eyes raked across Felicity's. She caught her breath. There was something in the way he looked at her, as if he was weighing her, and then found her wanting. Then he strode off.

"May all the saints bless you," the soldier called after him.

"Lady Felicity!"

She turned and saw that Sir Percy had finally reached her. "Your crown," he announced, holding his arm outstretched.

"Keep it," she said dismissively. "I no longer need it."

She could tell that she had puzzled him. But she did not care. Instead she wondered about the encounter she had just witnessed. Who was that gentleman, and why of all those present had he been the only one who heeded the beggar's cries?

And why had she felt so strange when he had turned his gaze on her?

The incident lingered in her mind, and she spent the next week searching for another glimpse of the mysterious gentleman. But he had disappeared, swallowed up by the vast metropolis that was London. He was not to be found in the crowds at Lady Fulton's ball, or at any of the routs or Venetian breakfasts that filled her engagement book. Nor was he among the select gathering that attended the opening of a new exhibit at the Royal Museum.

Finally she allowed another of her admirers to escort her to the opera, hoping that the gentleman would be there as well. Her companions raved over the exquisite singing, but she was unable to share their rapture, having spent most of the performance scanning the audience, hoping for a glimpse of the elusive stranger.

In the end she found him where she had least expected, within the sacred walls of Almack's.

"And how are you finding London this Season?" Mrs. Gilbert asked.

"Dull," Felicity replied succinctly.

Mrs. Gilbert gave a conspiratorial laugh. "True enough, although don't let the patronesses hear you, or they might consider it a slur on their hospitality. Still, it is hardly to be marveled at if one finds this Season lacking, compared to the grand celebrations of last year. After one has met the Tsar of Russia and his court, how could any other Season compare?"

The two women were sitting on one of the benches that lined the walls of the ballroom. Mrs. Gilbert was an older woman with whom Felicity had struck up a friendship. On the surface the middle-aged wife of a junior minister in the foreign service had little in common with a duke's daughter, but they both shared a taste for plain speaking, and a wry sense of humor. Felicity, although not yet one and twenty and still unmarried, had not made friends among the other unmarried young women who had come to London for the Season. Though the girls were her age or at most a few years younger, she felt separated from them as if by decades of experience.

Many of these young misses were experiencing London and the social Season for the first time. What could she find to say to these young girls? Felicity had traveled the globe with her father, an eccentric duke who had indulged his whim to see the world, and had seen no reason not to drag his daughter along.

At the age of eight she had been presented to Napoleon's court, during the short-lived Peace of Amiens. By the time she was eighteen, she had seen the great courts of Europe and the raw civilization that was America. She had ridden on camelback in the great desert of Egypt, and listened to her father declaim in Greek from the steps of the Parthenon in Athens. After all she had seen, a mere Season in London held neither wonders nor terrors for her.

Lady Felicity fanned herself idly, nodding to an acquaintance across the room.

"I vow, I never thought to see him here. I wonder what the patronesses were thinking," Mrs. Gilbert said.

Lady Felicity turned her head to follow her companion's gaze. She could see nothing remarkable, but then the crowd parted, and suddenly there he was, cool as you please.

Felicity felt her pulse quicken. "Have I missed something?" she asked.

Mrs. Gilbert made a discreet motion with her fan. "There, you see that gentleman? The one who just came in with Mr. Bingham?"

"Yes," Felicity said, her heart unaccountably racing.

"Well, that's Lord Kilgarvan. I must say I never thought to see him here, in Almack's of all places."

Neither had Felicity. The length of the room separated them, yet even at this distance Felicity could see that Lord Kilgarvan was not like the other gentlemen in the room. There was an air of surpressed energy about him, and tension. It was clear that he would rather be anywhere else than here.

"I have not heard of Lord Kilgarvan. Is he bad ton? Perhaps with a reputation for gambling or seducing young ladies?" Felicity asked, trying for nonchalance.

"No, nothing so shocking. But everyone knows that Lord Kilgarvan doesn't have a feather to fly with. His father left him saddled with debts."

"That makes him no different from many another nobleman. If solvency were a criterion for admittance, the ranks of Almack's would be thin indeed."

Mrs. Gilbert gave Felicity a sharp glance, as if sensing that her young friend had a more than casual interest in this stranger.

"Well, if he had an English title, or family connections, that would be a different matter," Mrs. Gilbert allowed. "But as it is he has naught to recommend him but an Irish earldom and an estate somewhere in the wilderness. He'll hardly find a bride among those here, no matter how charming the rogue looks when he smiles. No, he'll be better served by finding a wealthy cit who's willing to pay a fortune to see his daughter marry into the nobility."

Felicity glanced over at Lord Kilgarvan. It struck her then that of all those present the other evening, he had hardly been in a position to be charitable.

"I believe I would like to be introduced to this Irish earl," she said. "Can you arrange that?"

"Of course. But, Lady Felicity, are you certain this is what you want? The gentleman is hardly in your circle."

"Perhaps. Still he is the most interesting person we have seen all evening, and surely that is reason enough. There can be no harm in a few moments of conversation."

Mrs. Gilbert appeared to have her misgivings, but she rose and led Felicity over to where Lord Kilgarvan and Mr. Bingham stood. She presented Mr. Bingham to Felicity, and Mr. Bingham was pleased in turn to present his friend Lord Kilgarvan to the ladies.

Felicity took the opportunity to study Lord Kilgarvan, and was not surprised to find herself studied in turn. His black, wavy hair and dark eyes gave him the look of a pirate, and his countenance was carefully guarded. She could not tell what he thought of her.

Mr. Bingham and Mrs. Gilbert began chatting about common acquaintances, leaving Felicity and Lord Kilgarvan staring at each other somewhat awkwardly. There was much she wanted to say to him, but she did not want to do so in front of the others.

Just then the set ended, and a new set began, forming the quadrille.

"Is this your first time at Almack's?"

"Yes," Lord Kilgarvan replied.

"Then you must be sure to experience it to the full. Will you dance with me?" she asked, greatly daring.

He gave a small bow. "As you wish."

Taking her hand in his, he led her to the dance floor. She felt unaccountably nervous, as if she were a social novice, and not a veteran of a hundred balls.

The music began. Kilgarvan bowed to her, and she curtsied in return. Kilgarvan took her in his arms, as countless gentlemen across the dance floor did with their own partners, and Felicity realized that she had invited him to waltz with her.

Now that they were alone, she found that her courage had deserted her. She could not come out and ask him the questions that were burning in her mind.

She sought refuge in silence. He regarded her quizzically, and after a moment he spoke.

"Forgive my staring, but I cannot help thinking that I have seen you before," he said.

"Indeed," she said. "A few weeks ago, at the theater."

He shook his head. "I am sorry, but I do not recall."

"But I am sure you must. It was the most wretched Hamlet ever to disgrace the London stage.

"Ah. That I do remember."

As he smiled in remembrance she felt her innards contract, and she missed a step of the pattern. She could not believe a simple smile could be so devastating. Were he to smile more often he could have half the women of London at his beck and call.

But the smile was gone as quickly as it appeared, and she took a quick breath to steady her composure.

"There was a soldier that night. A beggar. No one seemed to see him, but you went up and spoke to him, and then gave him coins."

He shook his head in quick denial. "I don't remember that."

"But you did," she insisted. She could tell that he was lying. "I was there and I saw you."

He shrugged his shoulders, seeming to realize that there was no point in further denials.

"Surely you see beggars every day. What made you help him? Why that soldier?"

Her eyes caught and held his. The silence stretched between them for so long that she was afraid he wasn't going to answer, but she refused to give in. She did not know why, but she had to know the answer.

"He wasn't a soldier," Lord Kilgarvan said finally.

"But—"

"He was a navigator. He came over to work on the canals, and lost his arm when it was crushed in a rock slide. He found people were more apt to give charity to ex-soldiers, so he stole the soldier's coat off of some other unfortunate, and has been living in London ever since."

Most of the navigators who worked the canals were Irish laborers. It made sense that Lord Kilgarvan would feel sympathy for a fellow countryman. And yet . . .

"You knew he was a liar. But you still gave him alms?"

Lord Kilgarvan looked her straight in the eye. "The poor wretch was just trying to stay alive. Hoping to get home. There's no sin in that."

"Not many would have done as you did."

There was a wry twist to his lips. "I gave him enough coins for passage. No doubt he'll spend it all on drink, but that is his affair, not mine."

Gerald FitzDesmond, ninth Earl of Kilgarvan, looked down at his dancing partner, trying to hide his discomfort. His affairs were his own, and he was not prepared to discuss them with a woman he had known for scarcely a quarter hour. Especially not this woman. For Lady Felicity, with her regal grace and elegant carriage, was clearly one of the cream of English society. He did not know why such a woman would have sought him out, for it had taken no genius to realize that she had deliberately pursued the introduction. Left to his own devices he would not have approached her.

Not that an Irish nobleman wasn't worth ten or

twenty of his foppish English cousins. He knew his own worth and considered himself the equal of any gentleman here, and indeed better than most. It was not his character that was being judged here, however, but rather his purse and his prospects. And by that measure, he had no more hopes of marrying Lady Felicity than he did of marrying Princess Charlotte.

He glanced around the room. He had no doubt that within ten minutes of his arrival, his name, lineage and fortune had been known to every mother with eligible daughters, and every dowager who had taken a young relative in hand for the Season. And, as they judged such things, he knew he would not be considered a match for Lady Felicity. A duke's daughter, particularly one who possessed her full share of beauty and wits, could do far better for herself than a penniless Irish earl.

He had squirmed when she questioned him about the beggar. In truth he had remembered the man well. He told himself that the coins he had given the man, far more than he could afford, were no doubt wasted on drink. And yet a small part of him hoped that the man had done as he had promised, and had used the funds to purchase passage back to Ireland. At least one soul would be free of this blasted place.

When the dance finished, he bowed stiffly to his partner and surrendered her to another with a sense of relief. Suddenly anxious to leave, he sought out his friend Mr. Bingham, who was in the card room, deep in a hand.

As he entered the card room, Mr. Bingham caught sight of him and waved him over.

"Lord Kilgarvan, please let me make you known

to my friends. This is Mr. Blythe, and Mr. Abbott, and Sir Thomas Fortescue on my right."

The three gentlemen looked up as they were named, but it was clear they were far more interested in their cards than they were in making his acquaintance.

"Gentlemen," Kilgarvan said with a nod.

Mr. Bingham folded his cards and laid them down on the table. "And what did the Ice Princess have to say to you?"

"I beg your pardon?" Kilgarvan asked.

"Lady Felicity Winterbourne," his friend repeated. "The Ice Princess." He looked around the card table with a conspiratorial air. "I'll have you know, gentlemen, that the Ice Princess favored my friend here with a dance."

"Indeed!" said Mr. Blythe, raising his eyebrows.

Mr. Abbott pursed his lips and ostentatiously refolded his cards, clearly impatient at this interruption of the game.

"I'll say, I wish you the best of luck with her," Sir Thomas Fortescue said. "Had a go at her myself earlier in the Season. Nothing came of it, though. A few weeks of friendly acquaintance, and then suddenly she no longer had time for my invitations. She had moved on to other prey. Not that I was all that fond of her, mind you. Her tongue is much too sharp, and she's far too clever for her own good. But I wouldn't have minded getting my hands on that money."

He gave a deep sigh, as if mourning a lost love.

"It was a simple dance, nothing more," Lord Kilgarvan said, uncomfortable with the turn the conversation had taken.

"You two seemed to be chatting very cozily, for all that," Mr. Bingham pointed out.

He thought quickly. He had no wish to recount the story of the beggar, or of Lady Felicity's unusual interest in his act of charity. Especially since he still did not understand why she had sought him out.

"Lady Felicity was under the impression that we had met before, but since she has never visited Ireland, she realized she must have been mistaken."

"Hmmph," Mr. Abbott said. "Ireland must be the one place she hasn't visited. Chit has been everywhere else. I don't know what the duke was thinking, wandering off to foreign parts and taking his daughter with him. It just isn't natural."

"She's got all sorts of queer notions in her head," Sir Thomas Fortescue confirmed. "Always talking down to a man, just because he doesn't know the name of some Greek poet, or that New Orleans is in the Americas."

"No, it wasn't the travel that ruined her. It was the money. Fancy the duke leaving her all that blunt, and not bothering to tie it up as a dowry or put it in trust for her children. I mean, if you think of it, she has no reason to get married. She's probably holding out for a love match," Mr. Blythe said.

The gentlemen around the table nodded mournfully, sharing their distress at such feminine perversity.

A part of Kilvargan was still shocked by such frank discussion. Not that in Ireland it would have been any different. But in Irish society such topics were broached indirectly, discreetly, so that all could pretend that they weren't really being so vulgar as to discuss money.

Mr. Bingham smiled at his friend. "Well, there you are, Kilgarvan. Simply convince the lady that you are madly in love with her, until she agrees to marry you. You won't find a better catch anywhere in England."

"Thank you, but no," Kilgarvan said. "I fancy myself a wife who is a trifle more biddable. I have no wish to dance to Lady Felicity's tune."

Two

"How much longer do we have?"

Dennis O'Connor wrinkled his brow as he thought. "Two months. Three, if you're careful, though we'll be living on cabbage soup and old bones by the end of the third month."

It was hardly an exaggeration. Gerald FitzDesmond, Earl of Kilgarvan, looked around the tiny garret room that served as his lodgings. He had the honor of sitting on the bed, while Dennis perched on the trunk. A narrow window provided the faintest of illuminations, but it was enough. There was little else to see, save the grate in one corner, with a kettle next to it for boiling water. A makeshift clothespress held a wardrobe fit for a gentleman.

The wardrobe had been procured in Dublin, courtesy of his uncle, Mr. Throckmorton, who had agreed to finance this expedition.

The clothes were as out of place in this room as he and Dennis were. Kilgarvan knew he did not belong here. Not in this garret, nor in the finest town house in London. He belonged home, in Ireland.

Which was where Dennis should be as well. His friend was nearly of an age with Kilgarvan. Dennis's father had been the estate agent, and the two boys had grown up fast friends. Even now Dennis should be back in Kilgarvan, taking the place of the earl, and doing his best to stave off the inevitable disaster. But Dennis had been deaf to his arguments. If Kilgarvan was set on this London expedition, then Dennis felt it his duty to go along. Surely Kilgarvan was bound to fall into trouble without his oldest friend to guide him. Dennis offered to play the role of servant, valet and intelligence agent if needed. Kilgarvan had initially refused, but in the end he had given in.

"If you hadn't given that spalpeen two weeks' rent, there would be no need for worry," Dennis pointed out.

Gerald glared at his old friend. "You would have done no less," he said.

"What's done is done," Dennis said. "But how is the courting going? Did you see Miss Franklin at Almack's last night?"

"Yes, but she did not seem pleased to see me." Miss Franklin had been decidedly cool in her reception, refusing him the privilege of a dance, claiming that her card was full. Troubled by his encounter with Lady Felicity, he had not been up to the effort of charming Miss Franklin.

"Ah, well, there is always that Sawyer gel," Dennis said philosophically. "She seems eager enough. All you need to do is get her to the altar, and all our worries will be over."

Kilgarvan felt overcome by a sudden wave of self-loathing. "Of course. All I have to do is convince her that I love her madly, and she, and her papa's money, will fall right into my arms."

"Gerry," Dennis said, reverting to his childhood nickname. "You don't have to do this, you know. If we leave today we can be in Kilgarvan in a fortnight. Something else will turn up. It always does."

For a moment he was tempted. It had seemed such a simple plan, back in Ireland, when it was first proposed. Kilgarvan was young, handsome, unwed and with an ancient and respectable title. Why shouldn't he find himself an English heiress to marry?

But what he hadn't counted on was how much he would hate what he was doing. He felt like a prize bull being auctioned to stud. Or a slave trading his own freedom for that of his people, and the preservation of the Kilgarvan estate.

Ever since he left Ireland his thoughts had been confused. He no longer knew who or what he was. If only he could go back home, he knew he could recapture that sense of certainty. He closed his eyes and imagined himself standing atop King's Rock, looking down at the valley and the peaceful lake. The sun sparkled off the water, promising ease and rest to a weary traveler.

He opened his eyes. Kilgarvan was his, but not for long. Not unless he found a way to pay off the mortgages that his father had foolishly signed. An English bride was a small price to pay if she secured the land for himself and his people.

The morning after Almack's, Lady Felicity was enjoying a cup of hot chocolate in the blue sitting room while reading the London *Times*.

"Good morning, dear niece," the Duchess of Rutland said as she entered the room. Her brow furrowed slightly as she glimpsed the newspaper in Lady Felicity's hands. Reading a newspaper was hardly the mark of a young lady of distinction, but the duchess had long ago resigned herself to her niece's unconventional reading habits.

"Good morning, Aunt," Lady Felicity replied. The connection between them was actually more distant, the duke being her father's second cousin. But for simplicity's sake she had agreed to call them aunt and uncle. "I trust you enjoyed Lady Semple's soiree?"

"Immensely. It was a pleasure to renew our acquaintance. I find it hard to believe that her daughter, Miss Semple, is all of seventeen. She is an accomplished young woman, and was just presented at court." The duchess beamed as an idea came to her. "I should introduce you to her. I know you would like her."

"Perhaps," Lady Felicity said noncommittally. She had no intention of letting the duchess introduce her to yet another vapid young miss. The duchess was forever trying to fit Felicity into her idea of what a young woman enjoying her first London Season should be. Never mind that Felicity was nearly one and twenty, and had already been presented at the courts of Europe, not to mention enjoying the society in more exotic climes. The duchess still lived in hope that with sufficient encouragement Felicity could be made to fit the conventional mold.

It was not that she was cruel or unkind. That Felicity could have endured. It was rather that the Duke and Duchess of Rutland had been too kind, too welcoming.

It had been just over a year ago that her father had died of fever while they were visiting a friend's plantation in Jamaica. Felicity had coolly taken charge of the situation, made arrangements to have her father's body returned to England, and hired a companion to accompany her on the voyage.

Once she had returned to England she had journeyed to Rutland Hall to see her father interred next to his ancestors. Her very first callers had been the new duke and duchess, come to pay their respects.

They had been all kindness and politeness. Felicity was not to worry about anything. They were her family now and would take care of her. She would be as an older sister to their own young daughters. They would reside together at Rutland Hall during her mourning. And then, when the appropriate length of time had passed, they would introduce her to London society.

It was a shock to Felicity to discover that these strangers, whom she had never met in her life, now felt that they had the right, and indeed the moral obligation, to watch over her, and to tell her what she could and could not do. They were relentlessly inquisitive, kind and solicitous, when all she really wanted was to be left alone. She had lost her father, the one anchor in her world, the one person to whom she had felt connected. Now he was gone, and she did not know what to do with herself.

Nor did the new duke and duchess know what to make of her. She knew they would have been happier if she had been more like her young cousins, given to bursts of tears or extravagant declarations of gratitude for their kindness. She knew her cool reserve puzzled them, as did her insistence upon self-sufficiency.

The one saving grace was the terms of her father's will. The new duke had inherited the title and entailed properties, Rutland Hall among them. But to his only daughter her father had left the astonishing sum of two hundred thousand pounds. From this she drew a generous allowance, and when she turned one and twenty she would be given free rein to spend the money as she pleased.

Already comfortably wealthy even before inheriting the title, she knew the new Duke of Rutland did not begrudge her her inheritance. But she knew that he would have found her far easier to control if her inheritance had been left at his discretion. As it was, they had reached an unspoken truce. Lady Felicity was careful to observe the proprieties in public, and never to give offense. And in return, the duke forbore to criticize her choice of entertainments and friends.

"And did you have a pleasant time at Almack's?"

"The evening was tolerable."

"I regret that I could not escort you myself."

"Pray think nothing of it. Mrs. Gilbert was most pleased to have me join her party," Felicity said quickly.

"Well, tell me, who was there?"

"The usual set. Lady Alcock was there with her daughters, and the Misses Underhill. And Colonel Denham was most pleasant to Mrs. Gilbert and myself, and favored each of us with a dance."

"Was there no one else of consequence?" Felicity knew that her aunt was asking if there had been any gentlemen there who paid her particular attention. Colonel Denham was married, and thus could hardly be counted as a potential suitor.

"I did make a new acquaintance. Mrs. Gilbert was kind enough to present me to Lord Kilgarvan."

The duchess's face brightened. "Lord Kilgarvan," she repeated, tapping her lips with one finger. "Now, where have I heard his name . . . ?"

"He is from Ireland, newly come over for the Season. I understand that he is quite respectable, but his pockets are to let."

"Ah, that one. I have heard that he is as handsome as the devil himself, and far too proud for his own good." She gave her niece a sharp look. "I trust he did not put himself forward?"

Felicity knew she was being warned away from the handsome stranger. "You may set your mind at ease. Lord Kilgarvan was perfectly proper, and as you know, I am not the least romantical. I am hardly likely to lose my heart to a penniless Irishman, regardless of his appearance."

Far from being reassured by her words, her aunt seemed dismayed by Felicity's assurances. "You are such a practical girl," she said, but the thought did not appear to please her. "You know, there is no hurry in making your choice. You are a fortunate girl, and may take your time. If not this Season, then there is always the next. And I know Mary would be pleased with your companionship."

Lady Felicity doubted that very much. Mary was the oldest of the Rutland girls, and would likely resent sharing her first Season with her older cousin. Nor did Felicity relish the prospect. "You are all kindness," she said, but inwardly she vowed that she would marry Sir Percy Lambeth before she let herself return to Rutland Hall and another year in exile with these strangers who called themselves her family.

The duchess took a deep breath and changed the subject. "This evening Rutland and I will be dining at home, and then Mrs. Pelham has invited us to her rout. Will you join us?"

"That would be pleasant," Felicity said, although in truth she had already accepted an invitation to a card party. It did not matter. She would simply send a note, letting her hostess know that she had changed her mind.

She told herself that her decision to accompany her uncle and aunt this evening had nothing to do with the knowledge that Mr. Pelham had extensive family connections in Ireland, and that it was more than likely that Lord Kilgarvan would have been sent an invitation. Whether he would accept it she did not know, but she found herself looking forward to the evening with a sense of excitement that had long been absent in her life.

Gerald FitzDesmond had been in London for a scant two months, though in truth it felt as if it had been a lifetime. In these months he had learned many things. He had learned that a man was measured not by his character, but by his lineage and purse. That it was possible to be envied for his title and despised for his Irishness, and that there were people who held both opinions.

And he had learned that for unmarried women, the size of a girl's purse was in direct opposition to her comeliness. In fairness he allowed that this might not be a general rule, but rather his judgment might be colored by his limited experience in these matters. The crop this year might be scanty, the handsome girls having been snapped up the year before. Whatever the reason, he had found that those parents who were willing to receive his calls were possessed of the most unprepossessing daughters.

As if to mark his gloomy thoughts, he looked up and saw Miss Sawyer and her mother approach.

"Mrs. Sawyer. Miss Sawyer," he said with a bow. "How pleasant to see you."

"It is always a pleasure to see you, Lord Kilgarvan," Mrs. Sawyer replied. "Don't you agree, Prospera?" She poked her daughter in the side with her fan.

"Oh, yes. A pleasure," Miss Sawyer whispered, her eyes fixed on the floor, or perhaps on his shoes.

Mr. Sawyer had inherited a mill in Lancashire, which through dint of hard effort and canny business sense he had turned into a string of factories dotted across England, not to mention a substantial holding of gilt-edged government securities. Having grown wealthy beyond his wildest dreams, he had turned toward securing the future of his only child, Prospera. It was well known that Mr. Sawyer had boasted that though he was born in a cottage, his grandson would be of the gentry.

And then Lord Kilgarvan had appeared on the London scene, and within a fortnight Mrs. Sawyer had contrived an introduction. True, he was Irish, but he was an earl, and if Prospera married him, Mr. Sawyer could boast that his grandson would someday be an earl.

"The play last night was exceptionally fine. Prospera enjoyed herself most thoroughly. Our only regret was that you could not join us."

Somehow Mrs. Sawyer had contrived the loan of a box at the theater for yesterday's performance. She had sent him a note inviting him—no, verily bidding him—to join her party. The summons had had the feel of a trap closing around his neck, and so he had declined.

"I had a previous engagement."

Mrs. Sawyer's lips tightened. He knew she felt insulted, yet she would have to learn that he was not some lackey who would obey her every command.

"It is no matter. The Honorable David Pickering joined us, and he paid most particular attention to Prospera, so she did not suffer your absence."

He heard the veiled threat in her words. London gossip, as related by Dennis O'Connor, had it that the Sawyers had been close to accepting the Honorable David Pickering's suit. Then Kilgarvan had arrived in London, and the Sawyers appeared to be playing one off against the other in an attempt to bring Kilgarvan up to scratch.

"It gives me pleasure to know that you did not lack for company," Kilgarvan replied, disdaining such a transparent ploy. Did they think to make him jealous? "I'll wager that your party was far livelier than that at Almack's."

Mrs. Sawyer's eyes brightened at the mention of Almack's, as he had known they would. No doubt she was picturing herself and Prospera being received into the sacred halls of Almack's.

"Of course, we understand completely. A man of your rank has many demands on his time," Mrs. Sawyer said affably. "Is that not so, my dear?"

"Yes," Prospera replied, raising her eyes to his, and then dropping them self-consciously.

Mrs. Sawyer looked around, preening herself and making certain that all present saw her daughter being favored with the attentions of such a distinguished nobleman.

A wave of contempt swept over him, but he did not know who deserved it more: Mrs. Sawyer, for being willing to sacrifice her daughter to achieve her social ambitions? Or himself, for being willing to play this game, and to sell his soul to the highest bidder?

It was not that he disliked Prospera. It was simply that he did not know her. The girl was painfully shy, no doubt to make up for her mother's boldness. Prospera could turn out to be a pleasant, cheerful and intelligent girl. But the way things were progressing, he might not discover her true nature until after they were married. And even then, there was no certainty that once free of her mother's control Prospera would assert herself. Perhaps her mother would always be with them, an invisible presence, or worse yet, a visible presence.

A vision flashed through his mind of his wedding night. There was Prospera, modestly dressed in a cotton night rail, lying on the bed as if a virgin sacrifice. And there he was, naked, ready to ravish her. And then in his vision he heard a voice say, "My, his lordship is most well endowed—do you not agree, Prospera?"

A cold shudder of fear swept through him, and he closed his eyes to will it away.

"There you are, Lord Kilgarvan. I have been searching for you everywhere."

He opened his eyes to find that Lady Felicity Winterbourne had joined their circle.

"Pray make me known to your friends," Lady Felicity prompted.

"Lady Felicity, may I present Mrs. Sawyer and her daughter, Miss Prospera Sawyer."

The Sawyers curtsied, clearly overawed at having been introduced to one of the most celebrated women of this Season. He could see Mrs. Sawyer storing up every detail of Lady Felicity's appearance in her mind, the better to relate it to her acquaintances on the morrow.

"I hope you do not find me rude, but I promised

to fetch Lord Kilgarvan. My uncle, the duke, wishes to speak with Lord Kilgarvan to ask his advice about the Irish question and the bill that is before Parliament. I am certain you understand."

Lady Felicity linked her arm in his, then gave the Sawyers a dismissive nod. "If you will excuse us?"

She swept him away before the Sawyers could respond. She led him out of the main salon, into the hall that led to the drawing room. There he stopped, digging in his heels.

"I have no wish to discuss politics with Lord Rutland or with anyone else," he said stubbornly.

Lady Felicity smiled up at him. "Nor has my uncle any wish to discuss politics with you, sir," she replied.

"Then why did you fetch me?"

"You had the look of a drowning man," she said simply. "I could not leave you there."

He had been wishing himself anywhere other than there, yet it was strange that she had seen his distress, when the Sawyers had appeared to sense nothing of his inner turmoil. It was a lucky guess, or she understood him too well. And he wanted neither her understanding nor her sympathy.

"I did not need your help," he said.

"Fine. Then shall we return to the Sawyers? I am certain they would be glad of another coze with you."

He repressed the urge to shudder. "No."

"I thought as much," she said. "Now, come along. My uncle is in the card room. We can observe the play, and when a decent interval has passed, we can emerge, and your friends will be no wiser."

It was a good plan. And Mrs. Sawyer had been too clearly in awe of Lady Felicity to attempt to follow them into the card room.

"Lead on," he said at last. "But do you make it a habit of rescuing gentlemen in distress?"

"There is a first time for everything."

Three

Morning sunlight streamed through the windows of Felicity's bedroom, illuminating tiny motes of dust that danced in the golden shaft. The display caught her eye, and Felicity stared at the spectacle until a passing cloud robbed the sun of its brilliance. She felt a pang of disappointment, and then laughed as she realized how absurd it was to miss such a thing. The sun would be back, and the dust motes would dance again, if not today, then surely another day.

It was a sign of how heartily she was bored that she could find herself captivated by dust specks. Felicity rose from her seat at the writing desk and began to pace. She was restless, but she knew not what for.

Pacing soon lost its charm, for though the duke's London town house was on a scale that befitted his consequence, still this was London, and even the most spacious of bedrooms was ill-suited for pacing.

But she did not want to leave this room, for if she did, she risked encountering Lady Rutland, who would insist that Felicity join her in whatever plans she had for that day. And in truth Felicity was in no mood for either accommodating her aunt's wishes, or for the inevitable argument that would follow when she refused.

Crossing over to the mantelpiece, Felicity lifted down a small lacquer box, then sat down in a chair. Inside the box was treasure, although not the sort that most young ladies kept in boxes.

The box was filled with remembrances of her journeys. Dozens of seashells of all sizes lay inside, collected from the shores of more places than she could easily recall. Carefully she removed a brilliant pink shell and held it in her hand, running her fingers along its delicate ridges. She could remember when she had found this. She had been a small girl playing on the shores of a Greek island. She could no longer remember which isle it had been, but she remembered clearly the joy of discovering this most perfect of shells. How proud she had been when she had shown it to her father, convinced that this delicate opalescent shell was worth more than any gem. Her father had laughingly agreed with her, and encouraged her to keep her treasure and to search for more.

As she had grown older, she eventually realized that the shells had no real value, save as sentimental keepsakes. Still, she had continued to collect small shells over the years. And there were other treasures besides the shells. Reaching in the box, she withdrew an exquisitely carved jade elephant, scarcely bigger than her thumb, an Egyptian scarab, a scarlet feather from an exotic bird, three wooden beads, a set of jeweled combs, and lastly a child's ring of lapis lazuli.

She stared at the collection thus arrayed on her writing table. And there were other souvenirs that did not fit in the case, but which she had brought with her to London. A silk fan from Spain, a rug from Persia and a few small pieces of jewelry that her father had given her. Not to mention her ability to say "good morning," "good evening," "please" and "thank you" in a dozen languages.

It was little enough to show for all her years of travel. And yet each item held a memory. The jeweled combs had been the gift of Senhora Almadillo, who had lost her husband in the Peninsular War, and had set her sights on becoming the next Duchess of Rutland. Felicity had liked Senhora Almadillo, and would not have minded having her for a stepmama, but she had not been surprised when her father had chosen to end their stay in Lisbon, and thus the relationship. Her father had a knack for attracting women, but he soon grew bored and moved on.

She cast her mind back over the years. So many places, so many people. A week here, a few months there. Sometimes they spent an entire season in one place, such as the winter they had spent in Lisbon. But she had always known every place was impermanent. They could be settled for a day or a month; then the mood would take her father and he would announce, "Come along, puss. I have a mind to leave here, and it's time we were on our way." And then they would leave, with scarcely time to say their farewells. She had learned to travel with few possessions, for anything that could not be packed quickly was discarded and left behind.

Sometimes she thought of those friends she had made, and wondered if they ever thought of her. Or had she and her father been more like butterflies? Bright and gay, they had wandered into the lives of other people, and then flitted off again, leaving their acquaintances to resume their lives.

One could admire a butterfly for its beauty. But one could not touch it, nor could one grow to love it.

She shook her head, unhappy with the turn her thoughts had taken. She despised self-pity. With a quick sweep of her hand she swept the treasures back into the case, and then firmly closed it shut. The past was the past, she reminded herself. She could not change the past, but her future was hers alone to determine. She could mope here, miserable and alone in her room. She could stay on with her aunt and uncle, until advancing age rendered it acceptable for her to set up her own household.

Or she could do as generations of women before her had done, and seek out a man with whom to build a life. But she would not wait for the man to find her. She was tired of waiting for others to decide her future. She would choose her own husband and her own life. Never again would she permit herself to be dragged willy-nilly away from all she held dear.

Her feelings of restless dissatisfaction persisted in the fortnight that followed the Pelhams' rout. She tried to find solace in her usual activities, purchasing new books to read and new vocal music to practice. She visited Mrs. Dunne, whom she and her father had met in Ceylon, and chatted about mutual acquaintances and the changes that had occurred since her visit.

But nothing was enough to satisfy her. And she could barely tolerate the company of Sir Percy Lambeth. When his servile deference became too much for her, she had given him his marching orders. She was pleased to be rid of him, and realized it had been a sign of how deep her loneliness was that she had actually considered Sir Percy as a marriage prospect.

There was no lack of gentlemen eager to take

Sir Percy's place as her suitor. Felicity treated these
gentlemen with supreme indifference, showing no
one gentleman any sign of partiality. Well, that was
not precisely true. In these two weeks she had encountered Lord Kilgarvan more than once, and had
taken advantage of these occasions to improve her
acquaintance with the Irish earl. She found he had
a dry sense of humor that matched her own. And
unlike the fortune hunters who courted her so as-
siduously, Lord Kilgarvan was not afraid to argue
with her, or to point out when she was wrong. He
treated her with respect, but did not feign deference. And she liked him all the more for it.

By paying careful attention to the gossip, she had
learned a great deal about him. For all his title, the
earl was clearly not a member of the inner circle of
society. His title was suitably old, but suffered from
being Irish and thus not as good as an English title
would have been. His estates were mortgaged to the
hilt, but it was general knowledge that the debts were
the fault of the late earl, and that Kilgarvan was working hard to redeem them.

It was also common knowledge that he had come
to London to find a wealthy bride. Some scorned him
as a fortune hunter, but most avowed that such a
course of action was only common sense. And his
courtship of a cit's daughter was seen as confirmation
that he had a fitting sense of his worth and his place
in society.

Kilgarvan found Lady Felicity to be a welcome distraction from his courtship of Miss Sawyer. It was not
that his suit was going poorly; on the contrary it was
going too well. He knew that the Sawyers were waiting

for him to declare his intentions, and were somewhat puzzled by his delay. Each day he told himself that today was the day he would pay his addresses to her father, and secure her hand in marriage. But one day turned to another, and still he did not speak.

He knew his time was running out, along with the funds his uncle had lent him to finance his sojourn in London. The Sawyers were growing impatient. If he did not propose, he could lose her, and he had neither time nor money to begin courting another. He told himself that Miss Sawyer was everything that he had desired. She was young, wealthy, apparently biddable, and her parents were suitably impressed with his title. She was no beauty, but that could be a blessing, since it meant it was highly unlikely that another man would form a passion for her once he left his new bride in Dublin.

His logic was flawless, and yet still he could not bring himself to the sticking point.

He mounted the steps to the Dunnes' town house with a sense of trepidation. The Dunnes were hosting a poetry reading, and he knew that Mrs. Sawyer was planning to attend, no doubt eager to flaunt her daughter's artistic sensibilities.

Entering the foyer he gave his coat and hat to a footman, and then moved to pay his respects to his hosts.

"Good evening, Mrs. Dunne," he said with a bow.

"How pleasant to see you," Mrs. Dunne replied. "But I am afraid you will be disappointed, my lord. Mrs. Sawyer sent a note around earlier saying that she was unwell, and that she and her daughter would be unable to attend."

He forced himself to smile, although inwardly he was seething. He knew Mrs. Dunne was trying to be kind, but it was lowering to realize that she, like most of the rest of society, was treating him as if his engagement to Miss Sawyer was a foregone conclusion. "I am sure your other guests will provide sufficient diversion."

As he moved past Mrs. Dunne, he entered a brightly lit salon. Rows of chairs were arranged in artful groups facing the center of the room, where presumably the poet would stand.

A connecting door led to a room where refreshments had been laid out.

There were about three dozen guests. A small gathering for London, but Mrs. Dunne was an unusual hostess in that she preferred smaller groups rather than a giant squeeze. But it meant there was no chance that he could slip out before the readings began. Such behavior would be most discourteous, not to mention that it would be seen as confirmation that his only motive for attending had been to please Miss Sawyer, the presumptive Countess Kilgarvan.

He accepted a glass of punch from a footman in the vain hope that the alcohol would help smooth the edges of the evening. But the punch was heavily watered, fit for ladies or even children.

Wandering back into the main salon, he saw that Lady Felicity had arrived. She was chatting busily with two gentlemen, but upon seeing him she made her excuses and then wandered in his direction.

"I would advise against the punch. If I know Mrs. Dunne, there is nothing in there save fruit juice," she said by way of greeting.

He could not help smiling. "I had already concluded as much." He turned his head and with an eyebrow imperiously summoned a footman, and then placed the nearly full glass on the silver tray.

"So tell me," he said. "I have never been to a poetry reading before. What can I expect?"

"Heaven only knows," she said. "It depends very much on the poet. Alas, there are some unfortunates who can pen the most brilliant verse, but when they read their own work aloud it loses all sparkle. If we are lucky we can expect a brilliant evening. Or it may be the most tedious evening of your life."

A few moments later Mrs. Dunne began circulating through the crowd, urging her guests to take their seats. He held no high hopes for this event, but willingly guided Lady Felicity to a chair and sat next to her.

Her company was an unexpected consolation. He enjoyed being with Lady Felicity, because with her there was no need to carefully watch his every utterance and gauge his actions by her mood. They were clearly not a possible match, and without the need to court her he could be himself. And it was pleasant to have at least one acquaintance in London who did not seem to measure him by his Irish birth or his lack of fortune.

He did not know why Lady Felicity seemed to enjoy his company. Perhaps she was tired of the fortune hunters who followed her around. Or perhaps it was simply because he was a novelty. Whatever the reason, he was grateful for her friendship.

Once her guests were seated, Mrs. Dunne rose and made a short speech of welcome. Kilgarvan, along with the other guests, then applauded politely as Mr. Larkin took his place at the front of the room.

The poet's appearance was unprepossessing. A portly young man, his hair hung in long, flowing locks, but even the dimmest of eyes could see that the flaxen color of his hair was the result of dye.

The poet opened his mouth, and in a high, nasally voice said, "I will now read to you a selection from my narrative epic entitled *The Doomed Lovers,* a moral tale from the age of chivalry."

Each verse that followed was worse than the one before. Even the simplest of ideas was so wrapped in metaphors and allusions that it was impossible to make heads or tails of what the poet was talking about.

He glanced around and saw that the faces of those present held looks of rapt attention. At least, those present who still had their eyes open. One gentleman had fallen asleep, his head nodding on his chest. Kilgarvan looked over at Felicity, knowing she would share his distaste. Her eyes met his, and then she nodded.

"Come," she whispered.

He looked at her blankly.

She grasped his arm and then arose, and he was forced to stand with her. "Come," she repeated more loudly.

He could not believe he was doing this. Leaving in the middle of the recital was the height of rudeness. And yet he could not turn down the escape that Lady Felicity offered.

He followed her into the refreshments room.

"That, my lord, was one of the worst performances I have ever heard. I vow I could not endure another minute," she said with a shudder.

"Yes, but will not Mrs. Dunne take offense at your leaving so precipitously?"

Felicity shook her head. "No. It is one advantage of my upbringing. Mrs. Dunne will chalk it up simply as one of my odd starts."

"Your upbringing?"

"Come now, my lord. Surely you have heard the gossip about me? It is well known that until my return last year, I had spent scarce six months in England in the last eighteen years. My father dragged me off to all sorts of foreign climes, which has had an unfortunate effect upon my character. Naturally I am still sometimes confused by the rules of proper society," she said with a twinkle in her eye.

"I find that difficult to believe," he said.

She smiled with a sardonic twist to her lips. "In truth, the courts of Europe are far more rigid and straitlaced than we here in England. Why, in Spain a lady is rigidly chaperoned at all times until the day of her wedding. If we were in Spain I could not speak with you this freely unless you were my husband." She colored for a moment, as if her tongue had run away with her.

"I see."

"In any case, my foreignness makes a convenient excuse, and one I am loath to give up."

With nothing better to do, he fetched her a glass of punch. She grimaced, but then drank it.

"Mr. Dunne's study is just down the hall," she said. "I am certain he would not mind if you joined him. Or you could slip away, if you have another engagement."

"And leave you alone? How could I, after you have rescued me again?"

From time to time they heard the poet's voice rise as he read a particularly dramatic passage. They chatted together until there was a pause in the reading and they were joined by the remainder of Mrs. Dunne's guests.

Now that his company was no longer required, Kilgarvan prepared to take his leave of Lady Felicity. He wanted to be far away before the second reading commenced.

He was about to take his leave of Lady Felicity when one of the gentlemen who had been speaking with Felicity earlier came up to them.

Dismissing Kilgarvan with a glance, the gentleman spoke directly to Lady Felicity. "Lady Felicity, are you unwell? Surely there could be no other reason for your hasty departure."

"Not that it is any concern of yours, but I am quite well, thank you," Lady Felicity said, looking down her nose at the man. "But if I had stayed there a moment longer I was certain that I would be ill."

"Harrumph," the man said, clearly not sure how to react.

"I must agree with Lady Felicity," Kilgarvan said.

The gentleman turned and looked at Kilgarvan. "I should have known it was you who convinced Lady Felicity to commit such a faux pas. An appalling lack of manners, but what else would one expect from an uncouth Irishman?"

From the way he said *Irishman,* it was clear that the stranger intended it as an epithet. Kilgarvan's fists clenched, but he forced himself not to give in to his anger. He would not give the fool the satisfaction of knowing that his words had the power to wound.

"On the contrary, the Irish are well known for their appreciation of fine poetry. And as for manners, a gentleman would know better than to intrude where he was not wanted, or to offer insult to another gentleman."

"Well said," Lady Felicity added, turning so she stood by his side, so that they presented a unified opposition.

The gentleman looked from one to another. "I see I was wrong to hope for a civil conversation," he said, not bothering to conceal his sneer.

Four

Felicity could see anger in the set of his jaw, but Lord Kilgarvan said no more, merely watching as the man stalked off.

"Mr. Hackett was most rude," she said.

"He is not the first."

Lord Kilgarvan would not meet her eyes. He took a half step as if to move off, but she laid her hand on his arm, forestalling his departure.

"Why do they dislike you so?" she asked, genuinely curious. "It cannot be simply that you are Irish. I have met other Irish peers: the Duke of Leinster, Viscount Southwell; and, of course, the Duke of Wellington is from Ireland, is he not?"

Kilgarvan hesitated so long that she feared he would not reply. Then he drew a breath. "The peers you mention may hold Irish titles, but in their hearts they are English. They come to London for the Season, and send their children to schools in England. Like as not they have homes in England as well as in Ireland, and may set foot on their Irish property only for the sporting season. My family has always lived on our land, with our people. And, of course, my grandfather had the audacity to marry a Catholic girl, a mere commoner. There are many who hold that against us."

"So why did you come to England when you knew you would be insulted?"

His eyes locked on hers, daring her to remind him of his poverty. "Because I had to. And once I have accomplished my errand, I pray to God that I never have to return."

She admired his forthrightness. She could see that he was fiercely proud, but he did not make excuses for himself, nor did he try to hide his circumstances. She knew what it was like to be an outsider in London society—always on the fringes, never quite belonging. At least she had her rank and her fortune to smooth her path. Kilgarvan had only a petty earldom and his own strength of character to make his way.

A small bell rang, as Mrs. Dunne summoned those of her guests who had not fled during the intermission to join her for the second part of the poetry recital, but Felicity felt no inclination to join them.

"It seems an awful price to pay for securing your lands. Tell me, is it worth it?"

Kilgarvan looked at her in amazement.

"You would not understand."

"How can I, unless you give me a chance?"

"The English do not speak of land. They talk of property, as if it were a soulless thing, simply an entry in an account book or a stake to be gambled away on the gaming table. But it is more than that. It is not just the land; it is the people. Those who live there now, and all those who have lived there before me.

"The first FitzDesmond was a Norman knight, given an earldom for his bravery. For hundreds of years the earls of Kilgarvan have cared for their people and defended their lands. And my father's mother was a MacCarthy, the daughter of the Mac-Carthy Mor. The people of the valley have known me from my birth, and I know them. How can I let them down? How can I live with myself, knowing that I have not lived up to their expectations?''

''And yet your father squandered his inheritance—''

''My father was a decent gentleman. Just not a wise one,'' he said with a bitter twist to his lips. ''Kilgarvan was not rich, but neither were we poor. But my father wanted more, not just for himself but for the people. He hoped his improvement schemes would enrich the land, but instead they impoverished him and he was forced to seek a mortgage.''

''Because of your father, your family stands to lose their estates.''

''I know. And in the end he knew, and I think the knowledge killed him.''

''You must hate the land.''

''Hate it? How could I? Kilgarvan is the most beautiful place in the world. Nowhere else are the valleys as green, the lakes and rivers as clear, the people as warm and welcoming. There is nothing I would rather be than the FitzDesmond of Kilgarvan, no finer title than that of a just master and lord. I would do anything to save them . . . even take an English bride.''

The fierce passion in his voice stirred something in her. There was no doubt of his sincerity. In that moment she envied him with every fiber of her being. She would gladly trade every pound of her inheritance for the certainty that Kilgarvan possessed. Here was a man who knew who he was and where he belonged. She had not known that a person could be so passionate about a place.

She had not known what she wanted until she heard him speak. And now she knew that what she wanted more than anything on earth was to share the sense of belonging that he had.

"Marry me," she said without thinking.

"I beg your pardon?"

"Marry me," she repeated, putting all the recklessness that she had inherited from her father into that one simple phrase.

"Are you mad?" he shouted, so loudly that she saw heads turn in the salon.

"You are the one whose wits have gone begging," she said, angry that he had rejected her offer so quickly out of hand. "Did you not just say that you were prepared to do anything to save your land?"

He raked one hand through his hair. "You must be mad, or jesting," he said. "And I am not prepared to be the butt of your joke."

"I assure you I am in deadly earnest." She felt giddy with the knowledge of the risk she was taking, and at the same time felt a strange pleasure in seeing how completely she had thrown him off balance. Kilgarvan, who had never appeared at a loss for words, now gaped at her like a raw schoolboy.

"You cannot be serious."

She gathered her thoughts. She could not tell him her true reason. How could she say that she had fallen in love with a place that she had never seen? She would do better to stick to practical reasons that he would understand. "Why not? We are of similar rank, and both of an age to be married. Our reputations are good, and you are handsome, and I am not precisely an antidote."

She had hoped he would smile, but he still appeared grim. "Come now, there is no need to be modest. You know full well that you are considered one of the toasts of the Season."

"A title that has as much to do with my inheritance as it does my features," she said sharply.

"And that is another matter. Why would the richest catch of the Season want to marry an undistinguished Irish earl?" He surveyed her figure with uncomfortable frankness, his eyes lingering at her waist. "Could it be that you have some reason for wishing a hasty marriage? I assure you I am no fool, and will not accept a wife who comes to me carrying another man's bastard."

How dared he! She raised one arm to slap him for his effrontery, but he caught and held her wrist.

"If you think so little of me, then I withdraw my offer," she said.

He lowered her hand but did not release her wrist. His thumb traced idle patterns against the back of her hand, causing her pulse to race.

"I apologize," he said. "But you must admit your offer is most unexpected."

She nodded, her anger fading as she realized that what seemed so right and logical to her must seem like a mad start to him.

"Just tell me this," she said. "We are friends, are we not?"

"Yes, but—"

She cut him off, unwilling to hear the qualifications. "Then let go of your stubbornness, and tell me plainly. If you must marry, why not a friend? Or have you formed an infatuation for Miss Sawyer?"

Kilgarvan grimaced. "I bow to your logic," he said. Her excitement swirled, along with a rising tide of panic as she realized just what she had done. She had just committed herself to marry a man, someone she realized she hardly knew at all. A proper English miss would have never dreamed of putting herself forward in such a way. But deep inside, Felicity knew that she was taking the right course.

"You do not have to answer me tonight," she said. "But if you decide to accept my offer, you may call on me at my uncle's house in Grosvenor Square."

"His grace is unlikely to look kindly on me as a suitor," Kilgarvan said, revealing that he was taking her offer seriously.

"Nonsense," Felicity said firmly. "The match is a respectable one, and my uncle will be grateful to have me off his hands. You will be doing him a favor by taking me out of London and putting a few hundred miles between myself and his precious daughters."

Gerald could not help thinking that it must all be some strange dream, even as he mounted the steps of the Duke of Rutland's town house in Grosvenor Square. It seemed impossible that Lady Felicity, the prime catch of the Season, had proposed to him. Half-convinced that he had dreamed this, or that it was all some elaborate jest, he had not even confided in his friend Dennis.

As he mounted the steps he felt himself break into a sweat, which he knew came more from nervousness than the heat of the June sun.

A gleaming brass knocker in the shape of a lion glared at from the center of the door, but before he had a chance to use it, the door swung open, revealing a footman.

He resisted the cowardly urge to turn away, and

stepped inside. Inside stood another footman, a senior servant, judging by his livery. Gerald handed his hat and gloves to the first footman and then turned to announce his errand.

"Pray inform the Duke of Rutland that Lord Kilgarvan wishes a moment of his time."

"His grace is expecting you," the senior footman replied. "If you will follow me?"

His stomach tightened. So last night had not been a dream, after all.

Kilgarvan followed the footman up a flight of stairs and then down a corridor. At the end of the corridor the footman paused and knocked on the door.

"Come in," a voice called.

The footman opened the door, then bowed to indicate that Kilgarvan should enter. Standing just inside the doorway the footman announced, "Lord Kilgarvan to see his grace."

The Duke of Rutland nodded, and the footman withdrew, shutting the door behind him.

Kilgarvan glanced around the duke's study, which this room plainly was. Windows on two sides filled the room with sunshine, illuminating the darkly paneled bookcases and the deep mahogany of the duke's desk. Two high-backed chairs were positioned in front of an unlit fireplace.

The duke seemed out of place in the room. A middle-aged man, he had the beefy red face and rotund figure that fit the popular conception of a country squire, but seemed ill-suited for one of the highest noblemen in the land.

There were two chairs in front of the duke's desk, but Kilgarvan was damned if he was going to sit in one of them like some tradesman come for an interview.

"Thank you for seeing me," Kilgarvan said, advancing with a bow.

The duke looked him over, his eyes sharp and knowing beneath impossibly bushy eyebrows. He nodded, as if making his mind up about something.

"So you are the Earl of Kilgarvan," he remarked, rising from his seat. He came out from behind the desk and extended his hand. "Not at all what I expected, from my niece's description."

Kilgarvan shook the duke's hand, vaguely surprised by the courteous gesture. He wondered what Felicity had told her uncle about him.

"Come, sit," the duke said, indicating the chairs in front of the fireplace. "There's brandy on the table over there, if you'd care for a glass."

He did not want brandy, although if the duke had offered a jug of Irish whiskey, Kilgarvan would have been hard-pressed to refuse.

"Thank you, but no," he said. He waited until the duke had taken his seat, and then sat down.

"May I assume that Lady Felicity has spoken to you?"

"Yes," the duke said with a sigh. "Came to me this morning, she did, and said that you were to be calling to ask for my permission to marry her."

"Er, yes."

"Havey-cavey business this. Don't suppose it occurred to you to ask me first?"

Actually, no. How could it have? Lady Felicity had proposed to him. But he could hardly tell her uncle that his niece had committed such a shocking breach of manners.

"Things happened quite suddenly," he said, striving for diplomacy.

"So tell me, what do you have to offer my niece?"

It was a question that had kept him awake all night. What did he have to offer Lady Felicity? It was not that he doubted his own worth. In truth he knew himself equal to any English gentleman. But worth was measured differently here than it was at home, and he knew that by the standards of English society, his marriage to Lady Felicity would be seen as an unequal match.

"I will admit I have little to offer, save a similarity of minds and temperament. And, of course, the lands of Kilgarvan, along with a title that has been borne with honor for over six centuries."

"Not to mention a crippling load of debts," his grace observed.

He flushed. "I am certain Your Grace is well aware of my circumstances. Yes, there are debts, but once they are cleared, and with the proper investments, the land can be made to prosper again."

It galled him to have to admit to his relative poverty. He hated having to play the part of a beggar. He knew that if he had a dozen years he could bring the estate back to prosperity without the need for a fat dowry. But he did not have a dozen years or even a dozen months. He had less than three months before Lord Cranfield called in his mortgages, and the land would be lost.

"Humph," the duke said. "Felicity said as much when she told me of your suit. Still, she could look higher for a husband, even with her odd starts. I see no reason for her to choose so quickly."

"If Your Grace feels he must forbid the match, I would, of course, abide by your wishes." A small part of Kilgarvan hoped that his grace would indeed forbid the match. This whole situation made him uncomfortable. He felt out of control, and it was not a feeling he relished.

The duke regarded him sharply, and then smiled for the first time. "I believe you would, though most would call you a fool. But Felicity? If I forbid her, it would only make her more determined. No doubt she would convince you to take her to Gretna Green, and then where would we be? No, no, better to let her have her way than to have her disgrace herself with a runaway match."

"Your Grace knows best."

"Besides, she will reach her majority in a few months, and then she can do as she pleases. Not that she hasn't always done so." The duke rubbed his hands together. "I must tell you, I will be relieved when she is no longer my responsibility. You never know what she is going to do next. Kept my wife on pins and needles—I tell you that. Always worrying about what strange notion would come into the girl's mind, and what influence she was having on our daughters. No, no, I will be glad to be rid of that."

"I have never known Lady Felicity to behave other than with perfect propriety," Kilgarvan said, rising to her defense. It was nearly the truth, if one overlooked a few trifling matters, such as her being the one to propose the match.

"Of course, of course," her uncle said. "Anyway, it is not her fault. I place the blame on her father. What kind of man would leave his fine English estates to go wandering off to the far corners of the globe? And dragging his daughter with him, exposing her to the most uncivilized elements. It's no wonder that Felicity has picked up some odd notions of behavior."

Kilgarvan felt a pang of sympathy for Lady Felicity. It was clear that the duke, though not a cruel man, nonetheless considered his niece to be an unwelcome burden. He wondered if Felicity's eagerness for marriage stemmed from her wish to escape.

"Do I have your blessing to ask Felicity for her hand?"

"Yes, yes, I have told you as much," the duke confirmed. "Mind you, my man will want to meet with yours to discuss marriage settlements and the like. I would be remiss in my duty if I did not see that suitable arrangements were made for her jointure, and for the children, should there be an unfortunate demise."

"Of course." He had expected no less.

Five

Kilgarvan took his leave of the Duke of Rutland. As he exited the study, he saw a footman leaning against the paneled wall of the hallway.

"Lady Felicity would like a word with you, my lord," the footman said, hurriedly straightening up.

And he would like a few words with Lady Felicity as well.

"Lead on."

The footman led him upstairs to a small sitting room. The door was open, and he could see that Lady Felicity was inside, seated on a small sofa, reading.

The footman cleared his throat. "Lord Kilgarvan," he announced.

Lady Felicity laid her book down carefully, then looked up at him. She gave him a welcoming smile, much as if he were any casual acquaintance come to call.

"Thank you. That will be all, James," she said, dismissing the servant.

"Good afternoon, Lady Felicity," Kilgarvan said. He glanced at the book, surprised to see that she had been reading *A Tour of Ireland* by Arthur Young. So she thought to learn about his country, did she? It would not take her long to realize that the Ireland he knew was not to be found in any book.

"Good afternoon. I take it the interview with my uncle went well?"

"Yes."

She waved her hand to indicate that he should take a seat, but he did not want to sit. He was too restless to be still.

"Would you care for refreshments? Tea, cider or something stronger? My uncle's cellars are quite fine."

"No, nothing."

He looked at her, and then at the door, which the footman had left open. Walking over to the door, he closed it firmly. It would give the illusion of privacy, although he had no doubt that everyone in the household, from his grace down to the boot boy, knew precisely why he was here.

Crossing toward her, he rested one of his arms on the back of a chair. "His grace was kind enough to give us his blessing."

"Of course. I assume he also told you how relieved he was that someone had come along to take me off his hands?"

"He did not say that."

"Not in those precise words, but I will wager that the sentiment was there." Felicity gave an ironic shrug of her shoulders. "But I take no offense. Our temperaments were too dissimilar for us to rub along well together."

There was a moment of uncomfortable silence; then Felicity spoke again. "So now, why are you not happy? You have the look of a man who is having second thoughts."

"Not precisely," he said, wondering how to put his misgivings into words.

"Have you thought of some reason we will not suit? You can still cry off, and there will be no more said of the matter."

He could still cry off, she said, as if he were some nervous schoolgirl who did not know her own mind. He did not like the role that she had placed him in.

"Before we agree, I want to be certain we understand each other. This will be a marriage of mutual respect and friendship. A marriage of convenience, as it were."

"And?"

"I would not agree to this if I thought you had formed a *tendre* for me. A marriage where only one of the partners feels love is doomed from the start." He felt ridiculous even saying the words.

"I assure you, I am not the least romantical in nature," she said in far too cheerful a tone. He could hear the laughter that lurked behind her words. "A marriage of convenience is all that I seek as well."

Her answer galled him. There was no need for her to sound as if it was impossible that she had fallen in love with him. He had been told that he was quite handsome, and there was more than one woman in Kilgarvan who would be disappointed that his bachelor days were over.

He could not shake the feeling that there was something more to Lady Felicity's marriage offer than she had told him. But he dismissed such thoughts as pointless. Knowing that the marriage had been her idea, rather than his, had made him uncomfortable with the proposition. His current hesitation was simply a sign of how little he liked feeling that he had lost control.

He took a deep breath and thought of Miss Sawyer. Compared to Miss Sawyer and her esteemed mother, Lady Felicity was a paragon of virtue. He should be counting himself lucky, not looking to find fault where there was none.

"Very well then, Lady Felicity, I ask that you do me the honor of accepting my hand in marriage." Even as he said the words, he hoped fervently that he was not making the biggest mistake of his life.

"You honor me greatly, and I will be pleased to accept your offer," Lady Felicity said, as if the match had not been her idea in the first place. "And since we are to be wed, perhaps you should call me Felicity."

"Then you should call me Gerald."

He felt suddenly at a loss. This match was all that he had hoped, all that he had worked for over the last months. And yet Felicity's acceptance seemed more like a trap than the promised salvation. It was no wonder that the young bucks referred to marriage as a sentence for life.

"Your uncle suggested that I speak with you to set a date for the wedding."

"I am in no haste. It makes no difference to me if we marry tomorrow by special license, or in a year's time," she said.

He knew she was referring to his earlier insinuation that she was seeking a hasty marriage to cover a pregnancy. In his heart he did not believe that she would do such a thing, and yet it was the most logical reason he could think of for her to propose marriage to him, rather than to one of her numerous suitors.

"There will be rumors enough over the wedding. A special license would only add fuel to the fire."

She nodded. "Indeed. I am not averse to a suitable

period of engagement. But there is one condition. You are to remain in London while we are engaged."

"Why?"

"Because I will not allow anyone to say I have been abandoned," she said.

"I would not do that."

"Not willingly, no," she conceded. "But you have said yourself how little taste you have for life here in England. And if you were to return home, even for a short visit, you would find matters that needed your attention. And a short visit would stretch into weeks, and then I would have to count myself fortunate if you managed to return in time for the wedding."

He could feel himself flushing as he realized that there was a grain of truth in her words. Still, he would not let himself be dictated to. It would set a poor precedent for their marriage.

"I will remain in England," he said, wondering if she would notice that he had not promised to stay by her side in London. "And we will be married as soon as the banns may be called."

He could not afford to be away from Kilgarvan for the entire summer. Nor could he wait a year, as she had proposed. The mortgages would fall due in barely two months. And while some of his creditors might be willing to wait for payment, he could not delay them long. Better to be married now and to pay them off, rather than risk losing Kilgarvan.

"Three weeks from this Sunday will be the end of June, and near the end of the Season. That will suit me well."

And it would suit him. With luck he would be back in Kilgarvan by early July. That would give him most of the summer to begin the long-awaited improvements for the estate. Perhaps he could convince Den-

nis to return sooner to begin hiring workers and laying in the provisions they would need.

"If you will see that the announcements are sent
to the papers, then I will have Lady Rutland see to
the details. It is short notice, but once she is over her
fit of vapors I am certain that she will rise to the
occasion." Felicity paused, a crease appearing on her
brow. "Shall I send an invitation to your mother? Or
is there anyone else you would like to send for from
Kilgarvan?"

He shook his head. "My mother resides in Dublin,
with her sister and brother-in-law. But she is a poor
sea traveler, and will not wish to make the trip."

"If you give me her direction, I will invite her anyway, for courtesy's sake," Felicity said firmly.

"Do that." He smiled, thinking of the commotion
that the invitation would cause.

"Pray tell, what is so amusing?"

"I was just thinking how astounded my aunt and
uncle will be to receive the news of my wedding," he
confessed. "They had sponsored my trip to London,
but never in their wildest dreams would they have
imagined that I would return with a duke's daughter."

His mother's sister had married a Dublin mer-
chant. Mr. Throckmorton was a self-made man, and
very conscious of his common origins. Kilgarvan respected the man for his achievements, but found it
difficult to like him. Mr. Throckmorton had made
no effort to hide his low opinion of Kilgarvan's father
and his mismanagement of his inheritance. He had
invited the dowager countess to reside with him in
Dublin, less out of charity than out of his urge to
gloat that he could provide for her what her son
could not.

It had been Mr. Throckmorton who had financed his nephew's trip to London, saying that since a nobleman could not be expected to turn his hand to honest work, it was best that he find a wife who could support him. Kilgarvan could find no fault with his uncle's logic, but the man's condescending manner had stung his pride. This was one debt it would give Kilgarvan great satisfaction to repay.

The news that Lady Felicity Winterbourne was to marry Gerald FitzDesmond, Earl of Kilgarvan, took London society by surprise. Although perhaps *surprise* was too mild a word. Stunned shock was a better way to sum up the reactions of those who read the notice in the *Times*.

There were all the ingredients of high drama, or low farce. The handsome, impoverished earl was to wed the wellborn and well-dowered daughter of a duke. That alone would have been fodder for the gristmill, but the news that the wedding was in a mere three weeks' time was enough to set tongues wagging.

His first inkling of trouble came when he received a note from Mr. Bingham, a distant cousin who had introduced Kilgarvan to London society. Mr. Bingham congratulated Kilgarvan on his good fortune, calling him a lucky cur. In what Kilgarvan fervently hoped was a lame jest, his friend asked for the secret for courting heiresses, and closed with an offer to help Kilgarvan secure a special license, should he decide it prudent not to wait the three weeks for the banns to be called.

Along with the congratulations came scores of invitations to routs, balls, Venetian breakfasts and the like. Hostesses who had previously refused to ac-

knowledge his existence now vied for the chance to
host the couple whose names were on every tongue.

If left to his own devices Kilgarvan would have refused most invitations, but since Lady Felicity continued to go about in society, he found himself pressed
into service as her escort, on those occasions when
she requested his presence. Tonight they were to attend Lady Sefton's rout, and then make an appearance at a ball held by the Stanthorpes. Like most
routs, what should have been a glittering occasion
more closely resembled a cattle market, as too many
people crowded into too small a space. Ladies and
gentlemen in their finest evening wear jostled and
pushed each other as they ascended the stairs to the
ballroom, bumping elbows with those who were in
the process of trying to leave.

After a quarter hour, or perhaps longer, they
reached the top of the stairs, and entered the
crowded drawing room. It was stuffy and hot, and the
din of conversation was so loud it was a wonder anyone could hear themselves think.

He could not suppress the small shudder of panic
that overtook him as he surveyed the crowded room.
He hated crowds, hated the pressed-in, closed feeling
of too many people. His breathing quickened in his
mindless panic that the air would soon run out.

Felicity seemed to sense his distress. Linking her
arm in his, she gave his hand a quick squeeze. "We
will just pay our respects to the Seftons and then we
may leave."

He nodded, knowing it would take nearly as long
to fight their way back down the stairs as it had to
ascend. As they made their way through the crowd,
he could not help wondering what would happen if
one of the ladies were to faint. Would the press of

the crowd hold her body upright? Or would she fall to the floor and perforce be trampled?

Felicity led him through the crowd toward the tall windows at the far end of the room. The windows were open to the night breeze, and presumably that was where Lord and Lady Sefton were holding court. As they moved through the crowd, heads turned to follow their progress, and though conversations paused in their vicinity, the fierce whispers resumed as soon as they had passed.

He knew they were discussing Felicity and himself, and the rumors surrounding their engagement.

He looked over at Felicity, but she appeared as cool and composed as if she were carved from ice.

"How can you stand it?"

"I beg your pardon?"

"This. You know that we are the chief topic of conversation," he said.

Felicity lifted her chin with the haughtiness of a duchess. "They have been talking about me since the day I was born. They will most likely be talking about me long after I am in my grave. I do not pay it any attention, and I suggest that you do the same."

"I will try," he said.

But in the week that followed the gossip got worse. Dennis O'Connor, who was used to taking his daily pint in a tavern patronized by servants at liberty, at first denied all knowledge of the rumors. But then he relented, realizing that his friend needed to know what was being said about him. According to Dennis, the gossipers were divided into two camps. One camp held that Kilgarvan had compromised Lady Felicity, or that she had compromised him. The other camp was of the opinion that Lady Felicity was increasing, and was attempting to cover her indiscretion through

a hasty marriage. Several names were bandied about
as possible fathers of this mythical child, though Kilgarvan's was not among them. He, it seemed, was
merely a convenience, having agreed to take on Felicity and the child in return for her vast fortune.

The rumors made his blood boil, the more so because there was nothing he could do about it. If he
tried to proclaim Felicity's innocence, who would believe him? Moreover, would he believe himself? He
told himself that he had quashed the suspicions that
had arisen when Felicity first proposed this scheme,
and yet the gossip left him with nagging doubts.

He considered suggesting to Felicity that they postpone the wedding ceremony, but then thought better
of the idea. Suggesting a postponement would be an
insult to her, making it seem that he too had his
doubts about her innocence. No doubt she would cry
off, and then where would he be? He could hardly
begin courting another heiress, not after his name
had been linked to Felicity's.

No, for better or worse, he had to go through with
this marriage.

But after a week of increasing gossip, he had had
enough. While dining with a friend at White's, he had
overheard Lord Manley speculating on Felicity's mor-
als, or lack thereof. Kilgarvan rose from his table and
made his presence known, assuming that this would
end the matter. But it did not. Instead of apologizing,
Lord Manley leeringly congratulated Kilgarvan on his
good fortune, declaring that Kilgarvan was fortunate
not only to have found a wealthy wife, but one who
had been educated in her travels and must surely pos-
sess skills not to be found in an ordinary bride.

Cold rage filled Kilgarvan. Reaching down with

one hand, he grabbed Lord Manley's cravat and used it to haul the old lecher to his feet.

"Apologize. Now," Kilgarvan ordered, not loosening his hold on the man's cravat. His left hand clenched into a fist, and he struggled against the urge to rearrange the leering features with his fist.

Lord Manley's face began to turn purple from the pressure on his windpipe. Realizing he had misjudged the situation, the old lecher began babbling apologies.

Kilgarvan barely listened to what the man said. No mealymouthed apologies could make up for the slander he had uttered, yet what other choice did Kilgarvan have? Lord Manley was sixty if he was a day. Kilgarvan could hardly challenge the man to a duel.

"Enough," he finally said in a growl. He released his hold, and Lord Manley collapsed back into his chair.

Kilgarvan's eyes swept the gathered crowd. "Is there any other gentleman here who would like to comment on my nuptials or my prospective bride?"

His blood was boiling for a brawl, but he was not surprised that no one took up his challenge.

"Come along, Gerald," his friend John Bingham said. "There is no sense letting an old fool spoil your evening."

Kilgarvan remained and ate dinner, but he knew he was poor company, and after dinner he excused himself. As he returned to his lodgings, he realized that he could not endure another fortnight in London. Not unless he intended to spend it brawling and dueling every highborn English fribble and his brother.

It was better that he leave London for a bit and let things quiet down. It was unlikely that he would re-

turn to England in the near future, so he should
make the most of this visit. He would go see for himself the mills, and factories, and other great engines
of progress he had heard so much about.

In the morning he sent Felicity a note telling her
that he would be gone from London for a while. He
knew he should tell her in person, but having decided to leave, he could not wait until a civilized hour
to call. He was eager to flee this bustling metropolis,
to see what he could of the English countryside, to
breathe clean air again, and to stand where he could
see the land and was not constantly hemmed in by
stone and crowds.

If only it did not feel so much like he was running
away.

Six

Felicity was furious. How dared Kilgarvan leave London, with nothing more than a note? How dared he leave her alone to face down the rumormongers on her own?

She should never have let Kilgarvan goad her into agreeing to such a brief engagement. It had only given the gossips more grist for their mill. But she had never expected that their engagement would create such a controversy. Their union was seen not as a minor sensation, but as a full-fledged scandal, the details of which grew more outrageous with each telling.

And it was their misfortune that this Season had been particularly dull. There was no new scandal to distract everyone from her marriage to Kilgarvan, and as the wedding day drew nearer, the gossip grew ever more outrageous.

She knew Kilgarvan had found the gossip difficult to endure, but that did not excuse his leaving her to face it alone. Even a child knew that one had to face gossip head-on. Kilgarvan's disappearance was seen as confirmation of the worst of the rumors.

So much for his promise to remain with her. He had not returned to Ireland, but neither had he

stayed with her. She knew now what his word was
worth.

In the first days after his departure her anger
burned white-hot. If she could have found Lord Kilgarvan, she would have broken the engagement in
an instant, never mind the consequences to her reputation or his. In time society would forgive her, and
if Lord Kilgarvan could not find another bride, well,
he would have brought it on himself.

Eventually her temper cooled, and she realized
that she did not really want to call off the wedding.
She still wanted what Kilgarvan had: the security of
a place that was wholly her own. A chance to watch
the seasons come and go, and to really get to know
the people around her for a change. A chance to be
a part of a community, rather than merely an eternal
guest.

She could still have that with Kilgarvan. She knew
that. But she also knew that she needed to protect
herself. She had counted on Kilgarvan showing himself a reasonable man, willing to be guided by her.
The last week had shown this to be a foolish assumption. Now she needed to take steps to make certain
that her intended husband could not abandon her
lightly again.

That afternoon she left word that she wished to see
her uncle when he returned from his club. It was late
in the day when he finally sent for her.

After exchanging pleasantries, her uncle came
right to the point. "Still no word from that fiancé of
yours?"

"No, but I did not expect any," she said. "Lord
Kilgarvan has much to do if we are to be ready to
leave England after the wedding."

It was the same excuse she had repeated over and

over again for the last week. For all she knew, it might even be the truth. But she hated having to dissemble.

"Humph." Her uncle gave her a sharp look, but did not dispute the truth of her words.

"I do have a favor to ask," she said. "When the marriage settlements are drawn up, there are a few . . . conditions that I wish added."

"There is no need for you to worry over such things. I will make sure your interests are well represented. A suitable allowance for pin money, provisions for the children, and the like. You can leave it to me."

Her uncle's tone was sharp, as if she had accused him of laxness in his responsibilities, and she hastened to reassure him. "I know you will do what is best for me," she said. "But I am not quite comfortable leaving the bulk of my inheritance in Lord Kilgarvan's hands. He has done wonders with the little he has, but he has no real experience in managing capital. And given the example of his father . . ."

She gave a delicate shudder, as if the prospects were too horrible to contemplate.

"If you have such doubts, then perhaps it would be best to postpone the wedding. Or to cry off and tell Lord Kilgarvan that you have changed your mind. In a week's time it will be too late for second thoughts." There was a moment of silence, and then he added diffidently, "Just say the word, and I will take it upon myself to break the news to your aunt."

It was a kind and generous offer, and it warmed her heart. Lady Rutland had thrown herself into the wedding preparations with fervor, trying to compensate for the gossip surrounding her niece with the lavishness of the wedding preparations. It was clear that Lady Rutland could not wait to be free of the care for Felicity, and it would take a brave man indeed to inform Lady Rutland that Felicity had changed her mind.

"No, I do not wish to change my mind. I still think Kilgarvan and I will suit. But there is no harm in being cautious."

Her uncle nodded sagely, stroking his chin with his right hand. "I see what you mean. Lord Kilgarvan struck me as a responsible gentleman, and yet one can never be too careful in such matters."

In a few sentences she outlined her plan to her uncle. He agreed to add the clauses to the marriage contracts, but warned that Lord Kilgarvan was unlikely to view these changes well.

"You may leave that to me," she said.

Kilgarvan returned to London two days before the wedding was to take place. He had been away far longer than he had intended, and knew that Felicity was likely to be annoyed with him. He consoled himself with the knowledge that this had not been a mere pleasure trip. On the contrary, he had put his time to good use, going to Basingstoke to see the new canal being built, up to Birmingham to inspect their cloth mills, and over to Bedford to see the canal works. Everywhere he went, he had been impressed by the industry he had seen. England had moved forward into the nineteenth century, seizing the advantages of progress, while Ireland lagged woefully behind.

He vowed that Kilgarvan would not remain a rural backwater. Once he returned, he would bring the best of what he had seen, and put it to good use.

A note in his quarters directed him to call on Lord Rutland's solicitor to sign the marriage settlements.

As he entered the solicitor's offices, a young clerk greeted him, and asked his errand. Upon learning his identity, the clerk immediately showed him in to see the senior partner, Mr. Clutterbuck.

Mr. Clutterbuck proved to be an elderly man, thin and stooped as if he had spent his life bending over desks and papers. As Kilgarvan was shown in, Mr. Clutterbuck rose from his seat, using the arms of his chair to lever himself upward.

"Lord Kilgarvan, it is indeed an honor," he said, attempting a bow.

"Mr. Clutterbuck," Kilgarvan said, acknowledging the bow with a nod of his head. "I must apologize for not responding to your missive sooner, but I have been away from town."

"Of course. Quite understandable. Please have a seat, my lord." He waited until Kilgarvan had taken a seat, and then lowered himself slowly into his own. Then he turned to the young clerk. "The Winterbourne papers, William."

In a moment the clerk returned bearing a sheaf of papers tied round with a red ribbon. He handed the roll to Mr. Clutterbuck, and then took his leave.

Mr. Clutterbuck looked at him inquiringly. "I assume you will want to review these with your man of affairs?"

Kilgarvan repressed a smile. The nearest he had to a man of affairs was Dennis, his friend, valet and occasional voice of reason. But Dennis would hardly be of use in this situation.

"My family's affairs are handled out of Dublin," Kilgarvan said.

"Oh, quite. I had not thought of that."

"I am certain I will be able to review these for myself." He had never seen a marriage settlement before, but how complicated could it be?

Mr. Clutterbuck untied the ribbon with trembling fingers, and then handed the papers to Kilgarvan. "As you will see, my lord, there are a few conditions. Perhaps you could read it over, and then I can explain any parts that appear confusing."

Kilgarvan smoothed the documents out and began to read.

It was most enlightening. He learned that his intended's full name was Felicity Sarah Caroline Winterbourne, and that she would turn one and twenty in less than a month. His eyes widened as he saw that her dowry was nearly two hundred thousand pounds, far more than rumor had reported. In addition to sums invested in the funds, Lady Felicity had inherited shares in shipping lines and canal companies, had a respectable sum invested with the East India Company, and owned a copper mine somewhere in Wales. And those were just the major items. The full list of her interests covered more than a page.

He felt the first twinge of unease. He had no idea how to manage such interests. It had been naive of him to expect that Felicity's dowry would come wrapped up in a neat package. One did not keep two hundred thousand pounds in gold coins, after all. He reminded himself that there was no need for him to manage these affairs himself. He could hire a competent agent to manage these investments until he decided which ones to keep and which to sell off.

And then he came to the section specifying how the largesse was to be divided. There was a substantial but not unreasonable sum set aside for Felicity's personal use, for pin money and the like. Their oldest son would inherit Kilgarvan, but provisions were made to provide dowries for any daughters they might have, and a competence for the younger sons. An entire paragraph was devoted to describing the widow's jointure that Felicity would receive upon his demise.

All this was as he had expected, and represented the prudent provisions that he had expected the duke to make for his niece's marriage. But as he read the next paragraphs, his brow furrowed in thought as he puzzled out the legal phrases. Anger grew as he realized what Felicity and her uncle had tried to do.

He threw the papers back on the desk. "What is the meaning of this outrage?" he demanded. "Did you really think I would just sign this, like a lamb led to slaughter?"

Mr. Clutterbuck wilted under his wrath. "I admit the clauses are a trifle unusual—"

"Unusual? It's damn slavery—that's what it is."

"Perhaps you would care to discuss your concerns with his grace, the Duke of Rutland," Mr. Clutterbuck said in a quavering voice.

Kilgarvan rose. "Hardly likely. It seems Lady Felicity is calling the tune, so it is she whom I will see. Good day to you, sir."

As he stormed into the Rutlands' town house, he could not help remembering how nervous he had been on his first visit, only three short weeks ago. Had he known then what he knew now, he would never have come calling.

Lady Felicity was taking tea with her aunt. Both women looked up as he entered the room without waiting for a footman to announce him.

"Lord Kilgarvan, what a surprise to see you. When did you return to London?" Lady Rutland asked.

Felicity's eyes swept over him. She seemed to realize his anger. Turning to her aunt she said, "If you will excuse us, Aunt, I believe Lord Kilgarvan wishes to have a word with me in private."

Lady Rutland looked from one to another. "Oh, dear," she said. "I trust it is nothing serious."

Kilgarvan did not trust himself to reply.

Lady Rutland rose, and with a worried glance left the room. As soon as the door closed behind her, Lady Felicity fixed him with a fierce glare. "I thought we had an understanding," she said.

"So did I," he replied, taken aback by her vehemence. He was the injured party, not she.

"Then why did you abandon me here in London, to go gallivanting around the countryside like some schoolboy on holiday? Do you have any idea what it has been like this last fortnight?"

Her words pricked his conscience. "I didn't abandon you," he said. "There were things I needed to attend to before I left."

"And when did these matters come to your attention? Before or after you learned of the gossip?"

"I was only trying to protect you," he said. "I could see no way to put an end to the gossip, and I could hardly challenge every man jack in society to a duel. Leaving London for a while seemed the best course. For both of us."

His explanation seemed only to make her angrier. "I see," she said frostily. "You had such care for me that you left me on my own to face down London society—without any idea where you were, or when you would return. If you had remained, our engagement would have been a nine days' wonder. Your leaving was seen as confirmation of the very worst of the rumors. You are either the most selfish man I know, or a fool."

He hadn't meant to hurt her. He had been so happy to escape London that he had given little thought to how his actions would be construed. His sense of guilt warred with the sense of outrage that had brought him here in the first place.

"I apologize if you had to suffer any unpleasantness. I assure you, that was not my intention."

"I accept your apology."

"And I believe you owe me an apology as well, for the trick you tried to play on me."

"Trick?"

"Did you really expect me to sign those preposterous settlement papers?"

"They are more than fair," she said.

"Fair? It leaves me nothing at all."

She shook her head. "On the contrary, it gives you a great deal. Your father's debts will be settled, and the mortgages redeemed. Any personal debts you have will be settled as well; you merely need to give a list of your creditors to Mr. Clutterbuck and he will see to it."

"And this is supposed to please me? What about the rest of the dowry?"

Felicity gave a grim smile. "I did not deceive you. The funds are there, and you may have access to them. Upon my approval."

So she had known it all along. He had nursed some faint hope that the scheme had been instigated by her uncle, but Felicity's attitude made it clear that whoever had first thought of the restrictions, she was quite pleased with them.

"Why not simply put me in shackles and be done

with it? You do not want a husband, Lady Felicity; what you want is a lapdog."

"There is no need for you to take umbrage with me. Should your judgment prove sound, in a few years we can amend the terms of the agreement."

In a few years? She was crazy to think he would ever agree to such a thing.

"When have I ever given you cause to doubt my judgment?"

"When you left me," Felicity cried. Spots of anger dotted her cheeks, and her hands were clenched in anger as well. "If you do not like these arrangements, then tell me, and I will send the notice to the papers informing them the wedding is off. I understand Miss Sawyer has been taken off the market, but no doubt there will be another like her, whose family is too blinded by your title to see your character."

Every ounce of pride demanded that he put an end to this match and let Lady Felicity suffer the consequences of her own conceit. The words trembled on the tip of his tongue, but he did not utter them. Felicity had him over a barrel, and they both knew it. It was either marry Felicity or return to Kilgarvan in disgrace and stand by as the mortgage holders took away everything that he held dear.

"Very well, Lady Felicity," he said, stressing her title. "If this is what you want, then I will sign that bloody document. But know this: You have chosen this way to start our marriage. Do not be surprised to find that you are getting exactly what you paid for."

Seven

The wedding ceremony was held in the tiny chapel of St. Luke's. With so little time to plan the event, even Lady Rutland's influence had not been enough to secure the availability of the more fashionable St. George's. As a result, the ceremony was small and private by necessity, a fact that Lady Rutland deplored, but which pleased Felicity.

Felicity did not remember much of the wedding. She recalled standing in the rear of the chapel, wondering if she could bring herself to go through with the ceremony. What was she doing? She was putting her life, her happiness, in the hands of a stranger whom she did not know.

And yet, was she any different from any of the brides who had gone before her? Today, all across London, young women were marrying men whom they had met only this Season. Felicity, at least, had the security of knowing that she was not wholly dependent upon her husband. She had her own competence to fall back on.

Lady Rutland informed her when Lord Kilgarvan and his groomsman arrived. Felicity breathed a sigh of relief, even as she tried to convince herself that she had never really doubted that he would come.

Her uncle escorted her down the aisle, and then placed her hand in Lord Kilgarvan's. She felt herself tremble, and forced herself to hold her chin high, trying not to reveal how nervous she was.

Lord Kilgarvan was dressed in a dark blue coat and buff pantaloons. His appearance was all that was elegant, but his face could have been carved from stone. His eyes were hooded, giving no hint of his emotions. She could not tell if he was angry or simply resigned. He might have been a complete stranger to her.

There was only one moment when she felt a connection to him: when the minister instructed her to promise to "love, honor and obey" her new husband. Kilgarvan's eyebrow rose upward as she repeated the word *obey*. Her eyes met his, and for a moment she knew that he saw the humor in her promising to obey him.

The moment passed as swiftly as it had come. In no time they were accepting the congratulations of the attendants, and then being escorted to the vestry, where they signed their names in the marriage registry.

And with that, it was done, and she was now a married woman. The wedding party returned to her uncle's house for the traditional wedding breakfast. Dozens of guests who had not been able to fit in the chapel had been invited to the breakfast. Felicity stood next to Kilgarvan, accepting their congratulations. From time to time she took a sip of tepid champagne.

A sumptuous repast had been laid out, but there was no chance for the bride and groom to dine—not when so many present wanted to express their good wishes. Felicity endured it as well as she could, ignoring the speculation that she saw in their eyes.

Kilgarvan did his part, standing next to her, as rigid as a soldier on duty. From time to time he smiled, but she knew it was false, and wondered if her own smiles were so patently artificial. At last the crowds thinned, and there was no one to speak to except each other.

"How much longer are we expected to stay here?" Kilgarvan asked.

Her hand clenched on the stem of the champagne glass. "No more than an hour," she said after glancing at the clock on the mantelpiece. "Perhaps a little less."

Felicity regarded her champagne glass, and then set it down carefully on a small table. She had eaten little, and did not want to overindulge in drink. Not now. In an hour she would leave this house to begin her new life with Kilgarvan. She would be his wife, and he would have the right to do as he pleased with her body.

She felt a tingle inside her. She was prepared to do her duty, but very much afraid that she did not know what that duty consisted of. She had a vague, general notion of what went on. Lady Rutland had attempted to give her niece the benefit of her experience this morning, but her words had confused Felicity rather than helped her. The act Lady Rutland had described had sounded painful and terribly undignified.

She had seen couples in love, and her father's countless affairs. Surely no one would waste so much energy and emotion if the end result was as Lady Rutland had described. She must have misunderstood. Lady Rutland, for all her five daughters, could not have had very much experience.

And then, before Felicity quite knew what was happening, it was time to depart.

She went upstairs and changed into her traveling
gown. She was not certain what their destination
would be. Since the day of their quarrel she and her
new husband had exchanged only the barest of civili-
ties. It had been left to her uncle to tell her that
Kilgarvan planned to return to Ireland immediately
after the wedding.

Her uncle had arranged a post chaise to take them
to Holyhead, from whence they would sail to Dublin.
They would spend this night at an inn along the way.

Felicity made the final adjustments to her traveling
gown, and then turned around one last time to survey her room. On the floor were two trunks. A new,
modish trunk was filled with finery, including a lace
night rail intended for this evening. Next to it was a
smaller brassbound trunk. The brass had been
shined but could not hide the scratches, nor the scars
to the wood accumulated over thousands of miles of
travel. In the smaller trunk she had packed clothes
suitable for travel in rough country. From her reading and conversations with those who had visited rural Ireland, she knew that travel was often difficult,
but no more so than many a journey she had made
with her father. And no matter what hardships, this
journey would be a pleasure, for it would bring her
to her new home.

Her home. Not an inn, nor a rented villa, nor the
estate of a friend. No, for the first time she would
journey to a place that was to be hers for as long as
she chose. She did not know Ireland, and was a
stranger to Kilgarvan's home. But in time they would
become part of her, as she would become part of
them.

The celebration was still going on as she said her
farewells to her aunt and uncle. Lord Rutland as-

sured her that she would always be a welcome visitor, a sentiment her aunt echoed with only the barest prompting.

And then the servant handed her up into the post chaise, and Kilgarvan climbed into the seat across from her. And she was off to start her new life.

The coach rocked and swayed as they left London. The silence between them stretched uncomfortably. Kilgarvan looked across the carriage at his new wife. Lady Felicity returned his gaze with an uncertain smile.

"It is a pleasant day for traveling," she said.

"Hmm."

He glanced out the window, and indeed the sun was shining. Strange, he could have sworn it had been cloudy earlier. Or perhaps it had merely been his own forebodings that had colored the day. He had a wife, and now he realized he had not the least idea of what to do with her.

Or what to say to her. He was still angry over the marriage settlement, but they could hardly spend the rest of their lives quarreling. And it had been his choice to sign the settlement and to proceed with the marriage. He could have refused. But having taken her money, his honor required that he treat Felicity with courtesy and respect. Not affection, although perhaps in time their friendship could be repaired.

If he won her friendship, she would consent to change the marriage settlement and to set things right. As soon as the thought occurred, he banished it from his mind. It was bad enough that he had made a mercenary match. He would not scheme to win his wife's affections out of financial motives.

What happened between them next would set the tone of their marriage. It was important that he and Felicity reach an understanding before he left her in Dublin.

"You must be pleased to be leaving London," Felicity said.

"I confess, I have been longing for this day to be over."

Felicity blushed and lowered her eyes, looking anywhere except at him. He wondered what he had said to raise a blush in her cheek, then realized she must have thought he was anticipating the wedding night. "That is, I am pleased that we no longer have to be on display like creatures at the menagerie," he said, hastening to correct her impression. "Hopefully in our absence the gossips will find some other unfortunates to slander."

"No doubt," Felicity agreed. "We are lucky that Lady Rutland is such a fine hostess. Our guests will carry tales of her fine hospitality, and of our apparent harmony."

Apparent harmony. He could not tell if she was complimenting him on his performance, or subtly insulting him for failing to live up to her expectations. It was difficult to know when she was being sincere and when she was being mocking.

But he would have a lifetime to get to know her better. Or would they always remain strangers to each other, she in Dublin or London, and he in Kilgarvan, meeting only when required for social functions, or for the sake of their children?

That was, if there were to be children. With relations this cold between them, Kilgarvan was not inclined to claim his marriage rights. Especially not when he still did not trust his wife and her reasons

for wanting to marry him. Prudence dictated that he
wait a time to claim his privilege as a husband, until
he was certain that Felicity was not breeding.

And if she was? Well, he would cope with that unpleasantness when the time came. There was always
the possibility of a Scottish divorce. He would rather
bear the shame of such a divorce than let Kilgarvan
pass to an heir that was not of his blood.

They had begun their travel early in the afternoon,
and reached the village of Corby in twilight. As the
servants bustled about unloading the luggage and
unhitching the horses, Kilgarvan descended and
then helped Felicity alight from the carriage. The
cobbled courtyard was uneven, and Kilgarvan took
her arm as they walked into the posting inn.

The proprietor himself came out to greet them.
"My lord, my lady, I trust you had a pleasant journey?"

"Fair enough," Kilgarvan answered. The journey
had been only a few hours, but they had had a long
day before they had even started. He was bone-tired,
not having been able to sleep the night before. Judging from Felicity's white face and drooping eyelids,
she shared his exhaustion.

"Your rooms are ready, my lord, as you requested.
The finest we have, the finest in all of Corby, if I do
say so myself. My wife Betty will take you up. When
you're ready, you can come down to the private parlor for dinner."

Kilgarvan nodded, and then the innkeeper's wife
led the way up the stairs. She threw open the first
door on the left. "This chamber will be yours, sir,"
she said.

Kilgarvan glanced in and saw a spacious chamber,
furnished with a bed, nightstand, chair, and a table

and washbasin. There was a door in one wall that stood slightly ajar, revealing a glimpse of a room beyond.

The women continued down the corridor to the next room. "And this will be yours, milady," she said, opening the next door. Felicity's room was similarly furnished, with the addition of a dressing screen for privacy, and a large pier glass mirror.

Felicity's eyebrows rose as she surveyed the room.

"Is there something wrong, my lady?"

"No, I am certain everything is satisfactory."

The innkeeper's wife looked doubtful, but she managed a curtsy. "There is hot water in the jars, and if you need more, just send for it. The boy will be up with your trunks presently."

She backed out of the room. "My lord, my lady."

Felicity waited until the innkeeper's wife had left, then turned to him.

"What is the meaning of this?" she demanded.

"Of what?"

She waved her hand, indicating the room she stood in. "Separate rooms? We were married this morning, were we not? Or am I mistaken?"

She had expected to become his wife in truth. The thought gave him an odd ache in his chest. He had assumed that she would be pleased with his decision to wait. But it seemed he had mistaken his wife once again.

"We are both tired," he said. "And I thought, under the circumstances, as it were, that it would be best if we, er, if we delayed the wedding night."

"I see," she said frostily.

"We are still strangers," he hastened to explain. "We should take some time to get to know each other first."

She shook her head. "Don't try to make excuses for yourself. What you mean is that I am not good enough for you, although you have no problem taking my money."

Her words cut him like a knife. There was truth in what she said, and he felt like one of the lowest creatures on earth.

"I was thinking of you—"

"Your solicitousness overwhelms me," she retorted, appearing suddenly vulnerable. She blinked her eyes rapidly, but he could not tell if her tears were of anger or of disappointment. He knew only that he had failed her. What had seemed so right and logical earlier now seemed an act of unspeakable cruelty.

"Felicity," he said, reaching for her.

She slipped out from under his grasp, marching across the room and flinging open the connecting door. "Go," she ordered. "Do not expect to see me for dinner. I find I have a headache."

He looked at her helplessly. He did not know how to put this right. There was so much that was wrong between them. Making love to his wife, tempting though that was, would not make things right. He did not know if they could ever make things right.

She held the door open as he passed through it, into his chamber. "I will tell the innkeeper to send up a tray," he offered.

"No need. I am quite capable of seeing to it myself," she replied.

With that, she slammed the connecting door shut. He listened for a moment, but did not hear the sound of a bolt shooting home. Perhaps in her anger she had forgotten it. Or perhaps, despite her anger, a part of her was hoping that he would reconsider, and make her his wife in truth.

He went down to the tavern room. But no matter how much he drank, he could not erase the memory of the pain in her eyes.

Eight

Felicity spent her first night as a married woman alone and wakeful. Gradually, as her anger cooled, she realized that she had misjudged her new husband. She had known that he was still angry over the marriage settlements. And with that anger between them, would it have been right for them to consummate the marriage?

The laws of the church and society would have said yes, and if Kilgarvan had asserted his rights, she would have accepted his embrace—not simply out of duty, but as a way to bind him to her, and, yes, as perhaps the start of a new family.

She consoled herself with the hope that it was not lack of desire for her that had kept Kilgarvan from fulfilling his duty as husband, but rather his stubborn pride.

She did not regret her marriage, but wished with all her heart that she had insisted on a longer engagement. It was their seemingly hasty wedding that had led to the gossip, which in turn had led to the bitterness between them.

But that was behind her now. She had two choices. She could dwell in the past, using her hurt and anger as a shield against Kilgarvan. Eventually anger would become the pattern of their days, and there would be no changing it.

But instead she chose to put her hurt feelings aside and work to win her husband's affection and trust. She had enjoyed his friendship before. She felt confident that she could do so again, provided that she did not let Kilgarvan and his temper drive her off.

With this resolution made, she felt in better spirits. The Earl of Kilgarvan did not know what type of woman he had married, but she was bound and determined to teach him that he could not lightly set her aside.

The next morning she put her new resolution in practice. Arising early, she donned her traveling dress and then descended the stairs to the private parlor.

She opened the door and saw Kilgarvan inside, seated at the table. The remains of his breakfast lay on the table before him, and he held a newspaper in his hand.

Kilgarvan looked up from the paper and gave a start. Laying the paper down, he rose from the table. His body was stiff, as if braced for hysterics or recriminations.

"Good morning. It is a fine day, is it not?" she asked.

"Indeed."

The look of confusion on his face was priceless. Kilgarvan looked like a man who expected a tiger, only to find himself confronted by a kitten. She quelled the urge to laugh.

As she approached the table, Kilgarvan pulled out a chair for her to sit; then he sat again in his seat across from her.

She poured herself a cup of tea, then glanced at the bell on the table. "Is there time for breakfast? Or do we need to leave at once?"

"Please yourself. I did not expect you so early, so I left instructions that the post chaise should not be readied before nine o'clock."

Felicity lifted the bell and rang it, then replaced it on the table. In a moment a serving girl appeared in the doorway. "Porridge, please, if you have it. And muffins or toast, if they are fresh."

"Will there be aught else?" the girl asked. Apparently she had expected a countess to dine on richer fare, but Felicity knew from long experience that if she consumed a hearty breakfast now, she would regret it after a short while in a bouncing and swaying carriage.

"No, that will be fine."

The serving girl disappeared, and Felicity turned to face her new husband. "You will find I am an early riser," she said. "But I imagine there is much that we will discover about each other in the coming days."

Kilgarvan nodded, clearly not trusting himself to reply. He looked longingly at the discarded newspaper, but she would not let him escape so lightly.

"From Holyhead, we will sail to Dublin on the morrow—is that not so?"

"Yes."

"I have never been to Dublin, or to Ireland, for that matter. So tell me, what should I expect?"

"Rain."

Under her prompting he gradually expanded his single-word answers into entire sentences. Their conversation held little of the ease it had had in the days of their friendship, but it was a beginning.

* * *

The next day they sailed from Holyhead to Dublin.
The crossing was a smooth one. Kilgarvan, after his
dire predictions of an unpleasant trip proved false,
took care to assure her that the trip was seldom this
easy.

Felicity's resolution toward cheerfulness and equanimity was often put to the test. Even when pressed,
Kilgarvan refused to be forthcoming about his plans.
He described Dublin in great detail, painting the city
as a modern center of culture and business. He was
less forthcoming about his estate of Kilgarvan, describing it in only the most general of terms. She had
learned more from the guidebooks she had read.

She began to suspect that he intended for her to
make her residence in Dublin, while he traveled on
to Kilgarvan in the south. But, exercising her newfound patience, she decided she would not quarrel
with him until he actually raised the scheme.

They arrived in Dublin late the next day, and spent
the night in a hotel. The next morning Kilgarvan
informed her that they were to call on his mother,
the Dowager Countess Kilgarvan.

Felicity felt a pang of nervousness at the thought
of meeting his family. Would the countess approve of
her? Or would she take exception to her son's
choice?

A hired carriage was summoned for the journey.
Felicity drew back the curtains so she could see this
new city. Last night she had seen little except the
bustling wharves and the hotel. Now, everywhere she
looked, she saw signs of prosperity and progress. As
they drove down the wide streets, past carefully laid
out squares and manicured greens, she saw prosper-

ous shops and elegant residences, all built in the graceful style of the last century. The buildings were primarily brownstone, with ruthlessly scrubbed stairs and gleaming painted doors.

Kilgarvan cleared his throat, and she turned her attention to him.

"Perhaps I have mentioned this before," he began. "But I wanted to remind you that my mother resides with her sister and her sister's husband, Mr. Throckmorton."

Felicity nodded. "And will I have the opportunity to meet the Throckmortons today?"

Kilgarvan grimaced. "I do not know. Mr. Throckmorton has numerous business interests. It is possible that he may be at his offices today. I sent a note last night informing him to expect our visit today, but . . ." He shrugged.

How very interesting, Felicity thought. Clearly Kilgarvan and his uncle were not on the best of terms. She wondered what had caused such a breach. And she was curious about Kilgarvan's relationship with his mother. From what she had gathered, the countess had chosen to reside in Dublin since her husband's death, while Kilgarvan had stayed on the estate, occupied with the attempts to bring his land to prosperity. It did not sound like a close relationship.

And yet there was something in Kilgarvan's voice when he mentioned his mother that made her wonder how he felt about his mother's absence.

The carriage drove into a small square and halted before a modest three-story residence. There was nothing to distinguish it from its fellows save the color of the door, a deep marine blue, and the brass numeral twenty-seven affixed to the wall.

Kilgarvan helped her alight, and they walked together up the steps.

A maid met them at the door and escorted them to a small parlor. There were three people in the parlor—two ladies, one of whom had graying hair and a trim figure, and the other whose hair was darker brown and decidedly plump. But there was a certain resemblance in the shape of their faces, to proclaim them sisters. There was also a stout middle-aged gentleman with bushy eyebrows that contrasted oddly with his gleaming bald pate.

The gentleman rose, as did the older of the two ladies. "Dear Gerald, how good it is to see you again," she said. She stepped forward and took both his hands in hers.

She must be Kilgarvan's mother, for he kissed her on the cheek as he said, "It is good to see you looking so well."

The countess was a thin woman, nearly frail, with graying hair. Her eyes were tired, but her high cheekbones indicated that she must have been a beauty in her youth.

"May I present Lady Felicity Winterbourne? This, of course, is my mother, the Countess Kilgarvan," he said.

The countess smiled at her daughter-in-law. "Lady Felicity is now also the Countess Kilgarvan, is she not? But under any name I am pleased to welcome her to the family."

Kilgarvan looked embarrassed as he realized his mistake.

"I am very pleased to make your acquaintance, my lady," Felicity said.

"Please, you must call me Eleanor," the countess

urged. "And this is Mr. Throckmorton, my brother-in-law."

"Your servant," Mr. Throckmorton said.

"And my sister, Mrs. Frances Throckmorton."

"Charmed," Mrs. Throckmorton said.

Kilgarvan and Felicity found seats for themselves, and the company resumed their seats.

The ladies chatted pleasantly for a few minutes, Mrs. Throckmorton inquiring about the London fashions, while the countess delicately probed Felicity regarding her background.

"You must excuse my curiosity," the countess explained. "It is just that my son is such a poor correspondent. He wrote little of you until the note he sent announcing your engagement."

Mr. Throckmorton snorted. "What my sister-in-law means to say is that your wedding came as quite the surprise, my boy. Thought you were all set to marry that Sawyer chit. You could have knocked me down with a feather when I heard you were to marry a duke's daughter. I thought you had decided to marry someone of solid worth, rather than a flighty noblewoman who most likely expects you to keep her in the highest style."

Such an insult could not pass unchallenged.

"Uncle—" Kilgarvan began.

Felicity placed her hand on his arm, forestalling whatever reply he intended to make.

"I do not believe that Kilgarvan owes you any explanations, and I most certainly do not," Felicity said frostily. "It is but for you to wish us to be happy, and to have the common decency to keep any reservations to yourself."

Mr. Throckmorton's monstrous eyebrows drew together as he attempted to stare her down. Felicity returned his stare, not breaking her composure. After what seemed like an eternity, Mr. Throckmorton was the first to break eye contact. "You have spirit—I will say that for you," he said.

Felicity realized that his words had been a deliberate test to see how she would react. Miss Sawyer would have fled the room in tears, but she was made of sterner stuff.

"My father raised me to know my own worth, and to speak my mind," Felicity replied. "And I have always found plain speaking is the wisest policy. Since you are a man of business, I am sure you would agree."

Mr. Throckmorton looked from her to Kilgarvan and back again. "Stubborn, that's what you are. And proud. Just like my nephew here. Never takes a word of advice from anyone. I begin to think you may suit him after all."

"Thank you," Felicity said, as if she had just received a great compliment.

The dowager countess broke the uneasy silence. "Tell me, how long will you be in Dublin? Your note did not say."

"I will be returning home presently," Kilgarvan said. "But Felicity—"

"Our plans are not yet fixed," Felicity interrupted. She knew Kilgarvan had been about to say that she was not to accompany him. She had no wish to quarrel with her husband in front of her new relatives, but neither would she let him assume that she was willing to remain behind.

The meeting with his family had gone better than he had hoped. Felicity had charmed his mother and his aunt. And as for his uncle, he had expected Mr.

Throckmorton to dislike Felicity, as a product of the useless titled classes. Indeed, his uncle's cutting remarks had come as no surprise. Kilgarvan, all too aware of how much he owed to his uncle's charity, would never have dared speak to him as Felicity had done. But rather than being offended, Mr. Throckmorton appeared delighted to find Felicity a woman of spirit. He'd even taken Kilgarvan aside when they were leaving, and complimented him on finding a wife of such good sense.

It seemed Felicity had the power to charm everyone in her circle. Everyone except him, that was. He wondered how she would take the news that he planned to leave her behind in Dublin.

He broached the subject that evening, as they were dining at their hotel.

"I must admit, I had not thought to find Dublin such a modern and fashionable city," Felicity remarked, delicately spearing a piece of fish with her fork. "But I suppose I listened too much to my aunt, who thinks that the world revolves around London and the Season."

"Indeed, I am glad to hear you say so," he said, seizing the opening she had provided. "You will find that Dublin society is the equal of any. My mother will be happy to introduce you, and I think you will find it quite diverting."

"I am sure Dublin can be quite pleasant. But I had thought you were quite anxious to return to your estate. Or do you intend to linger in Dublin?"

He glanced down at his plate. A salmon stared up at him, its glassy eyes seeming to reproach him for what he was about to propose.

"There is much that needs to be done in Kilgarvan. And, of course, the servants will have much to do to make the great house habitable again. So I think it best if you remain in Dublin for the summer, while I see to the renovations."

Felicity laid down her knife and fork. He braced himself for an explosion, which did not come.

"I see." She gave him a look that seemed to bore right through him. He felt guiltily aware of how eager he was to be free of his unsettling wife. And while it was true that Arlyn Court would need much work before it was fit for a lady's residence, he knew that it was not the reason why he wished her to remain in Dublin.

Felicity's presence, with all the attendant awkwardness, would only prove a distraction when he very much needed to focus all his energies on his estate. It would take years to bring Kilgarvan to rights, but after waiting so long, he begrudged every day that he had to wait.

He knew this, and yet there was a part of him that still felt as if he was running away.

Felicity shrugged her shoulders. "Very well, if that is what you wish, then I will remain in Dublin. I am certain I can find something to amuse myself. Although I would have thought that you would find the arrangement inconvenient, I suppose you know best."

"Inconvenient?" What could be more inconvenient than their present arrangement, which forced them into a pretense of domestic harmony?

"Certainly. After all, you will need to return to Dublin to secure my approval for your projects. Of course, you could write to me, but then if there was anything that was unclear, or if I had any suggestions, then I would need to send a return letter, and you would need to write back, and . . ." She shook her head. "I really think it a most awkward and bothersome arrangement, but if this is what you want . . ."

It took a moment for her words to sink in. "What do you mean, your approval?"

A waiter cleared their plates and brought the next course, a fricassee of veal. Felicity waited until the waiter had left before replying.

"Any expenditures for the estate require my approval. You do remember the documents you signed, do you not?"

She couldn't do this. She wouldn't. "This is blackmail!"

Heads throughout the dining room turned to stare at them.

"No, my lord, this is what you bargained for. You did not acquire a bank account. You acquired a wife. And now you have a choice. You can leave me in Dublin, or take me with you to Kilgarvan and convince me of what needs to be done."

Anger roiled inside him as he realized how neatly she had him trapped. There was nothing he could do. He needed her agreement to release the funds from her dowry, and if he left her in Dublin, he knew full well that no matter how many letters he sent, or how many pages of explanations, that there would be no funds forthcoming.

He wondered why she seemed so bound and determined to stay with him. He had done nothing to encourage her; on the contrary, after the last days he had been sure she would be glad to be rid of his presence. And yet she seemed determined to bedevil him. Was this some subtle form of revenge for the hurt he had inflicted on their wedding night? He tried to read her face, but he did not see triumph, merely determination.

He lifted his napkin from his lap and threw it on the table. In a breach of courtesy he rose, not caring that the meal was only half over. "You know I cannot gainsay you," he said. "But I tell you, it is a miserable journey. Before you are ten miles out of Cork City you will be wishing you had the sense to follow my good advice."

"Nonsense. You will find that I am a far hardier creature than you give me credit for," she said.

He glared at her, but she seemed immune to his displeasure. He strode off. As he left the dining room, he saw Lady Felicity calmly signaling to the waiter to bring her more wine.

Her icy calmness infuriated him, and he promised himself that he would make her regret her attempt to force herself where she was not wanted.

Nine

Kilgarvan and his new bride spent a week in Dublin. He chafed at every minute of delay, and yet there was so much to be done. He and Felicity met with the bankers who would oversee the trusts that had been established, and then he interviewed solicitors to find an agent to handle his affairs. The process would have been concluded sooner, but Felicity had objected to the solicitor he had chosen, claiming the man was too young and inexperienced, and so Kilgarvan had to begin the selection again. Finally a Mr. Perry was chosen as acceptable to both of them.

Mr. Perry's first task would be to redeem the mortgages, and then to draw upon Kilgarvan's accounts to pay off his other debts. Including the debt to Mr. Throckmorton. Kilgarvan spent a day closeted with the solicitor, until he was certain that both he and Mr. Perry understood the full extent of his financial situation.

In the end it was both better and worse than he had supposed. The money he had received in the marriage settlements would clear the mortgages and his personal debts, and leave a balance left over for the day-to-day running of the estate. But for any significant improvements or projects, Kilgarvan would

Patricia Bray

still need the concurrence of his wife to release the funds.

Such a reminder of his situation made him short-tempered, but Felicity seemed unaffected by his moods. She treated him with equanimity, suffering his occasional outburst with the patience of a parent humoring an ill-tempered child. But the more she exercised her patience, the more frustrated he became.

From Dublin they sailed to Cork City. There he made one last attempt to persuade Felicity to stay behind.

"I do not understand why you wish to come with me," he said.

"I have my reasons."

"It will be a miserable journey. Once we leave Cork City, the roads quickly dwindle to mere donkey paths. Inns and decent houses are few, and when we cross the Bheara Mountains, we may not count on even these for shelter. It is scarcely a trip for a lady."

Felicity merely raised one eyebrow and gave him a smile as if she could see right through him. "Your mother made the trip, did she not? Or did the countess arrive by heavenly chariot?"

Her barb hit home. "My mother has not been to Kilgarvan for nearly a decade. Even then the journey was a difficult one, and without funds for upkeep, the roads have grown steadily worse."

He complimented himself on his quick thinking. And his explanation was true, in a roundabout sort of way. He had not exaggerated the condition of the roads. The trip from Cork City to Kilgarvan was one only the hardiest of travelers would attempt.

Of course, there was another way. One could sail to the mouth of the Kenmare River and disembark at the town of Nedeen. From there the journey to Kilgarvan was still difficult, but far shorter. Not that Kilgarvan would have chosen that way himself. He'd had business in Cork City, and he'd made the difficult journey over the Bheara Mountains on more than one occasion. He knew he could make the trip in far less time than it would take to wait for a ship bound to Nedeen. If Felicity could not keep up, so be it. He would send her back to Cork City with a clear conscience.

But his wife was not so easily dissuaded. "I daresay if you can make the journey, then so can I," she said. "It will not be the first time I have traveled in rough conditions. And it will be worth it to see my new home."

He felt a sudden stab of apprehension as he heard her say the word *home*. Kilgarvan was not her home. It was his—his and his people's. And yet Felicity was a force to be reckoned with. He was already handicapped by her control of his purse. Who knew what schemes she might come up with once she was in Kilgarvan? She could easily upset his carefully made plans.

But he could not say no. Not when Felicity held the upper hand. All he could do was try to discourage her. "It will not be as you are used to. There is no grand society, no neighbors for a day's journey, save the local people. There are many projects that will need my attention, and I will have little time to keep you company. Even Arlyn Court needs restoration to make it habitable."

"All the more reason for my presence," Felicity countered. "If you are busy with the estate, then I must be there to supervise the renovations on the manor."

He ground his teeth in frustration. Why couldn't she see reason? Any sensible woman would have eagerly remained behind, after the grim picture he had painted. Yet the more obstacles he put in her path, the more determined Felicity was to accompany him.

"At least let me journey ahead and begin the work," he temporized. "And then you can join me in a few months, once things are more settled."

For a moment he thought it might work. But she shook her head no.

"Are you ashamed of your home?"

"No!" The question was absurd.

"Then you must be ashamed of me. Is that it? Are you so ashamed of your wife that you are afraid to introduce me to your people?"

"Of course not." But how could he explain what was truly troubling him? It was not that he was ashamed of Felicity, but rather that he feared her influence. Living with her, day and night, it would be hard to keep to the vows he had made not to consummate the marriage until there could be no doubt of the paternity of his heir.

It was a hellish bargain he had made. He had sold his soul to save his land. He had given up his own freedom, knowing that doing so would preserve Kilgarvan. But he had not counted on having to share Kilgarvan with his new wife.

"Then there can be no real objection to my accompanying you on the morrow, can there?"

She had him trapped, and they both knew it.

"I bow to your superior logic, madam," he said frostily. "We will leave tomorrow at first light."

"I will be ready," she promised.

She smiled at him, the picture of cool, well-bred elegance.

He tried to comfort himself with the knowledge that he still had one more card up his sleeve. Only he knew the route to Kilgarvan, and he would pick the most difficult path he knew. Surely after a day or two of discomfort his wife would be inclined to see reason.

But looking at his wife's self-confidence, he had the terrible lurking suspicion that nothing short of a plague of locusts would deter her from her goal.

On the morning they were to depart, Felicity rose early and breakfasted alone on a tray sent to her room. She knew that her husband was liable to be in a foul temper, and she was in no mood to humor his crotchets.

She did not understand the reason for his obstinacy. She had accused him of being ashamed of her yesterday, but even as she said the words she knew they were not true. If he was ashamed of her, he would never have introduced her to his family, or pressed so hard for her to remain with them in Dublin.

But if he was not ashamed of her, then what was his motive? Did he simply long to be free of her presence and the reminder of the mercenary bargain he had made? Or was there something more? Was there something or someone at Kilgarvan that he did not want her to see? And yet when he spoke of his land it was with such love and pride that she could not understand why he would not want her to see it.

Her imagination conjured up myriad explanations for his behavior, each more outrageous than the last.

Perhaps Kilgarvan was in fact a prosperous estate, and Kilgarvan's tales of poverty were a ruse. Or maybe Kilgarvan was already married, and when she arrived she would find herself confronting his common-law wife, and their dozen children.

Of course, that would mean that he had found a woman who was willing to put up with his ill temper and capricious starts. After these last weeks Felicity very much doubted that there was a woman in the civilized world who would cheerfully link her fate to that of the Earl of Kilgarvan.

Still, she set aside her misgivings and paid no heed to her husband's attempts to discourage her. On the contrary, his attempts served only to increase her determination. She would brave the Irish wilderness and prove to her husband that she was no hothouse flower. And perhaps, in time, they would rekindle the friendship they had once shared.

And she would see the country of Kilgarvan, the land that held such a firm grip on her husband's soul. Love for his heritage had driven him to sacrifice his pride and independence. She had not known it was possible to feel such an attachment to a place. But then, even in her childhood she had known that it was no use forming deep attachments to a people or a place. For nothing in her life had been permanent, no presence had been constant save that of her father.

She had loved her father, and had learned to endure the constant upheavals and to find what fleeting pleasure she could. As she grew older she understood some of her father's restlessness. But out of their wanderings had been born the desire for a place she could call home, a place where she felt she truly belonged.

Her husband had that sense. She could hear it in his voice every time he spoke of Ireland, in the way his eyes had shone when he had described his home. And just as she worked to win Kilgarvan's affections, she hoped to win a place for herself at Kilgarvan.

"What shall I do with this cloak, my lady?"

The maid's voice broke into Felicity's thoughts. She turned and saw the maid holding up a traveling cloak of light wool.

"Roll it and place it in the saddlebags, near the top, if you please," Felicity replied. She was certain to need it. Rain was the one constant in Ireland. All of the guidebooks had been quite emphatic on that point. And it seemed the farther you traveled from civilization, the more likely it was that the hapless traveler would be deluged.

The maid nodded and obediently placed the cloak in the saddlebags.

Felicity glanced around the room to make sure that nothing had been left unpacked. Besides the cloak, the saddlebags held two changes of wardrobe, her toiletries, and lastly her keepsake chest, wrapped carefully in oilskins.

Kilgarvan had warned her that they would be traveling on horseback, and she had made her preparations accordingly. Only those items essential for travel had been packed in the saddlebags. Everything else that she had brought with her was to be left behind, to be sent on to Kilgarvan by donkey cart.

"Have the saddlebags brought down," Felicity instructed. "And the trunks should be put with Lord Kilgarvan's until they are called for."

Felicity pressed a few coins into the girl's hand.

"Of course, my lady," the maid replied, hastily bobbing a curtsy.

Felicity left her room and descended the stairs. She made her way to the small door that led to the courtyard, then paused as she glimpsed her husband.

Kilgarvan was standing, talking to an ostler who held two saddled horses. Even she had to admit her husband cut a fine figure. He had put aside London clothes for dark breeches, a linen shirt and a plainly cut wool jacket. He hadn't bothered with a hat, and his jet black hair glinted in the sunlight. The ostler must have made a jest, for Kilgarvan grinned, his face reflecting a contagious enthusiasm. And then he caught sight of her standing in the doorway, and all trace of amusement fled.

As Felicity made her way across the yard, she saw her husband survey her appearance from head to toe. He scowled, and she knew it was because he could find nothing to fault. Like her husband, Felicity had shed her aristocratic finery for simpler garments more suited to travel. She wore a dark green riding habit, whose skirts were divided for convenience and narrow enough that they did not drape excessively over the saddle, and thus were not likely to be caught on brambles. On her feet were half boots that had been made for her in Portugal and recently resoled in London. She could walk all day in the boots, if need be. She had done it before.

Kilgarvan gestured toward the two horses he had purchased the day before. One was a chestnut, and the other a gray. Of average height, they appeared sound enough, if a trifle barrel-chested. Perhaps there was some mountain pony in their ancestry.

"I could not find a mount trained to the sidesaddle," her husband said.

She bit back a smile. Did he really think her so

feeble? "I prefer a man's saddle. Especially when the roads are uncertain," she replied.

A serving boy brought over her saddlebags. She waited while these were secured to the gray, and then Kilgarvan's own gear was secured to the roan. As she had guessed, there was no sign of a pack animal or a baggage cart. Kilgarvan intended that they travel lightly, indeed.

"There is still time to change your mind," he said.

"Have no fear," she replied. "I will not slow you down."

They set off on their journey, leaving behind Cork City, with its canals and industry. As they passed the ancient city walls, the cobblestone streets turned into gravel beneath their horses' hooves. Buildings became smaller and farther apart, and beyond them Felicity could see the rolling green hills for which Ireland was famed. Within an hour, the city had dwindled behind them.

Now the road was a dirt lane, although still well maintained. Beyond the hedgerows were fields, interspersed with clumps of small cottages with whitewashed walls and straw thatch roofs. There were other travelers on the road: a farmer leading a donkey cart, a young boy driving half a dozen pigs, and a laborer carrying his worldly possessions tied to a stick he carried over his shoulder. Each of these offered a cheerful greeting to Kilgarvan, which he returned. She knew that neither she nor her husband looked anything like an earl and his countess, and amused herself by wondering how the natives would have responded had she insisted on traveling in all her London finery.

They spoke little, but that suited her. She saw no need to fill the silence with empty words. But she could not resist stealing a glance at Kilgarvan when she was certain that his attention was elsewhere. There was something different about him today, and not simply because he had chosen to dress more simply. No, the change had more to do with the set of his shoulders and the way he held his head. It was in his eyes, and how the lines on his face seemed to have melted away.

And it was in the way he responded to each person who greeted him. Not that he had not been courteous in London. Rather, he had been all that was correct. But now when he paused, there was a smile on his face. It struck her that her husband was happy. For the first time since she had known him, he was at his ease.

Just then he turned his head, and his gaze locked with hers. He had caught her staring at him, and unaccountably she felt herself blushing.

"You see that line of clouds over there?" he asked, raising his left hand and gesturing with his whip toward the mountains in the west.

She nodded. She had had her eye on those clouds for the past quarter hour.

"I think it will rain," he said dolefully.

"I will not melt," she replied mildly, hiding a smile. Did he really think a little rain would be enough to make her turn back?

But he simply shrugged his shoulders, as if to say that whatever happened was her own fault, and returned his attention to the road. Her horse fell into line a little behind Kilgarvan.

Heavy gray clouds covered the sky faster than she would have believed, and a gentle rain began to fall.

Any hope that this was a passing shower soon passed as the rain intensified, and she could feel her riding habit becoming soaked through.

Taking the reins in one hand, she reached back and began fumbling with her saddlebags with the other. But she could not work the unfamiliar buckle with only one hand, and her efforts caused her horse to stop still, turning his head to stare at her reproachfully.

"Hold a moment," she called out. She swung out of the saddle without waiting to see if Kilgarvan had heard her. Looping the reins around the saddle, she then turned her attention to the saddlebag. With both hands it was easy to attack the buckles. She threw open the flap, musing that she was sadly out of practice. When traveling in the Peninsula she had become an expert at retrieving any item from a saddlebag while still on horseback. Her year in England had made her soft, and her skills rusty.

Throwing open the flap, she reached in and removed the cloak that had been packed only that morning. Before she could unroll it, the rain began to fall in sheets. A gust of wind blew her hat from her head, and her hair was soon plastered to her skull.

"Blast!" she swore.

Unrolling the cloak, she wrapped it around herself, placing her arms in the shoulders and then tying the strings of the hood beneath her chin. But she knew it was no use. Even as she refastened the buckles on the saddlebag, the torrential rain was working its way through the wool cloak and the riding habit beneath. Rivulets of water ran down her face.

At least it was July, and not the depths of winter, she consoled herself.

"I told you it was likely to rain."

She whirled and saw that Kilgarvan was standing next to her. He, too, had dismounted, and had donned a coat against the rain. He looked as drenched as she, but there was a certain satisfaction in his eyes.

She laughed, overcome with the absurdity of it all. "Rain, yes," she agreed. "But a second flood? Surely not even you could arrange such a thing."

Kilgarvan blinked, and she knew she had surprised him. A part of her was pleased that she could amaze him. But a larger part was hurt by his continuing assumption that she was a frail and delicate female, no different from any other gently bred lady. Didn't he remember any of the stories she had shared with him in the days of their early friendship? Had he dismissed them out of hand as exaggerations? Or, worse yet, had she meant so little to him that her confidences were soon forgotten?

She glanced around, but on this barren stretch of road there was no cottage to be seen, not even a copse of trees under which to take shelter.

"Come now," she said. "We can stay here and be soaked, or press onward. Surely there will be a shelter ahead."

"There was a farm not a mile back," he offered.

She shook her head. "No. If we turn back now, like as not you'll have me in Cork City before sunset. No, we ride on. Unless you mind a little Irish rain?"

He doffed his hat, sweeping it out in an elaborate bow. "As my lady wishes," he replied.

Then they remounted and continued on in the rain.

* * *

They rode through blinding sheets of rain for well over an hour before they came to the village of Drisheen. Located on a crossroads, the village boasted a small inn, where they had taken shelter from the storm. Kilgarvan could not remember when he had last seen such a storm. Even now, sitting inside the public room, he could hear the rain lashing against the windows of the common room and beating on the slate roof above.

Still, he had naught to complain about. Having changed his attire, he was blessedly dry, and as warm as a turf fire and a glass of hot whiskey could make a man.

A pot of tea rested by the hearth, waiting for Felicity's return. She was still upstairs, no doubt trying to remedy her appearance. By the time they had reached Drisheen, the pair of them had appeared much like a pair of drowned rats, earning clucks of sympathy from Mrs. Murphy, who ran the tiny inn.

Through it all, Felicity had remained in good spirits. He could not deny her that, though he shuddered to imagine how any other woman would have reacted in such a situation. In all honesty, he had to admit he had been looking forward to the rain, certain that a little wetting and a journey on muddy roads would make Felicity long for the comforts of civilization. Instead she had laughed at the weather, and pressed on with a cheerful determination that equaled his own.

He had underestimated his wife. It had become a habit with him.

He heard footsteps, and turned to see Felicity enter the room. She had changed into a simple muslin dress, and her damp hair had been braided so it hung down her back. She looked absurdly young and strangely vulnerable. He felt a pang of unease as he tried to reconcile the woman standing before him with the iron-willed termagant who was trying to rule every facet of his life through her purse strings. He shook his head, unable to bring the two images together in his mind.

"You will feel better when you have had something to drink," he answered. Rising from the bench, he retrieved the teapot and poured her a cup.

She cradled the cup between her hands, as if to warm them. She took a sip, and then looked at him with a quizzical expression.

"I suspect the good Mrs. Murphy took it upon herself to add a little Irish poteen to that tea, to warm you up, as it were," he said.

She nodded, then took another sip. "Well, if it is the custom . . ."

"It is."

The common room was simply furnished with a couple of chairs in front of the hearth, and two long tables with benches on either side. Pewter tankards lined the mantel over the fireplace, and for all its plainness, the inn was spotlessly clean.

Felicity sat in one of the chairs, still cradling the teacup with her hands. He took the chair opposite.

"Mrs. Murphy poked her head in a moment ago to assure me that dinner was on its way," he said.

Felicity looked out the window. "There are still a few hours of daylight. The storm may yet break."

"We will stay here for the night." He had hoped to make another ten miles today, but there was no sense in continuing on in this weather. Not now, when he had realized at last that nothing, not even an Irish gale, would sway Felicity from her determination to accompany him to Kilgarvan.

"I must admit, I expected rain, but hardly this torrential downpour. Are such storms common in the summer?"

"No, I have scarcely seen the like, myself."

"Such storms are reserved for English tourists, no doubt. You know for a moment there, I half suspected you of conjuring up the storm as a means of discouraging me." She smiled and arched her eyebrows.

He shook his head in denial, although he could not help thinking that if he had had the power, he might have tried the trick.

"Well, now you know that mere storms and poor roads will not frighten me off. What will you try next?" she asked, choosing to make light of his attempts to leave her behind.

"Highwaymen?" he suggested with a grin.

"Surely not!"

He could not lie to her. "Alas, highwaymen haunt civilized roads, where there is profit to be found. There is little danger that there are any to be found between here and Kilgarvan."

Of course there was always the chance that some fool would take it in his head to relieve an English traveler of the heavy burden of any riches he might be carrying—purely in a spirit of helpfulness, lightening the traveler's load, as it were. Hard times brought even the best of men to desperate measures. But even if such rascals had taken to plying their trade in the Bheara Mountains, Kilgarvan was too well known for any to risk attacking him or his wife.

"Good," Felicity said. "Not that I would allow the threat of bandits to discourage me, but I have already encountered more than enough of that breed to last me a lifetime."

It took a moment for her words to sink in. "When did you meet bandits?"

"Portugal. Or I believe it was Portugal, but it may have been Spain. There was much confusion over the precise location of the border between the two, you know."

He hadn't known, nor did he really care whether there was a border dispute in far-off Portugal. "When was this?"

"Half a dozen years ago, or thereabouts."

She had been a mere child. "And you saw bandits?" he asked, already knowing that it would not be a tame sighting that Felicity had to relate.

"Yes, I saw them."

He breathed a sigh of relief, but her next words stopped him short. "I could hardly help seeing them, as they kidnapped my father and me while we were journeying to Senhora Almadillo's estate in the country."

"You were kidnapped?" It was not quite a shout.

She leaned forward and patted his arm reassuringly. "Do not fret yourself. It was a long time ago, and indeed I was in no danger. Kidnapping there is quite common. It is almost a sport with the local bandits. They treated us with great courtesy. My father wrote a letter to his friends, and within a few weeks the ransom was paid, and we were set free."

He swallowed. He did not want to imagine what would have happened if the ransom had not been paid, or if the bandits had been less inclined to treat a young English girl honorably. What had her father been thinking, to put her in such danger?

"What was your father thinking?" he asked aloud.

"He thought it a great lark. It made a wonderful

story, and he often recounted the tale to our acquaintances."

He could not imagine why anyone would take such a risk with their own life, let alone with the life of their child. He doubted very much that this was the only danger Felicity had faced in her years of travel. No wonder she had seemed so eager to leave London, where the worst danger was a social snub, and the greatest excitement was to be the first to share a scandalous on-dit regarding one's acquaintances.

"I begin to see I may have underestimated you," he said, voicing aloud the thought that had occurred to him with more and more frequency over these last days.

"Indeed," Felicity replied, inclining her head to accept his tribute. "But what will you do now?"

It was blindingly obvious that he had mistaken the character of his wife. Felicity was neither a schemer nor a sheltered English lady. On the contrary, she was a strong-willed woman, and one who had shown remarkable forbearance, considering how hard he had tried to leave her behind.

"Shall we start over?" he asked. "I know I have been a poor companion these days, but I would beg your pardon and ask that we start again as friends."

Her eyes searched his face, and then a small smile touched her lips. "That would please me very much," she said.

Ten

The next morning, the sun sparkled off the rain-soaked fields as they left the town of Drisheen. True to his promise, Kilgarvan put aside his pride and bitterness over the marriage settlement, and tried to begin afresh with his wife, as if they were strangers who had met for the first time the day before. For her part, Felicity seemed more than willing to put aside her own hurt feelings.

Each mile they traveled brought him closer to his home. From time to time he would point out scenic views, or share bits of local legend. Felicity listened intently, and occasionally shared stories of her past and journeys she had made. At other times they would travel in companionable silence, secure enough not to feel the need to fill the air with idle chatter. And somehow he found himself telling her more than he had intended, sharing his plans and dreams for the future.

Each night they stayed at an inn, or availed themselves of the hospitality of the local gentry. He was not surprised to find that word of his marriage had gone on ahead of him, and those of his acquaintance were quick to congratulate him on his good fortune.

By unspoken consent there were only two subjects

that Felicity and Kilgarvan did not broach. The first was the subject of the marriage settlement. The second was the fact that despite being married for nearly a month, they were still husband and wife in name only—a fact that grew more and more irksome to him, and more awkward to explain, as their hostesses appeared surprised by his request for separate bedrooms.

Not that he did not desire his wife. On the contrary, each day he was with her it grew harder and harder for him to control his wayward thoughts. It had been easier to ignore her when she was Lady Felicity of London, all polished elegance and cool perfection. Then he'd admired her beauty dispassionately, as one might admire a porcelain statue.

The woman he traveled with was a different matter. This Felicity was warm, human, and with her wind-tousled hair and sun-kissed complexion she was infinitely more desirable than any London beauty. Her eyes sparkled when she laughed, and he found himself telling the most outrageous of stories for the simple joy of hearing her laughter.

At night, when he lay awake, unable to sleep, he reminded himself of the reasons why he had not consummated their marriage on that first night. But his logic, once compelling, now seemed the arguments of a fool or a craven. He had grown to know Felicity, and while he still did not understand all the reasons why she had proposed marriage, he did not doubt her essential honor and truthfulness. If Felicity had found herself with child, she would have taken responsibility, and not tried to trick a man into marriage.

And his other reason—wishing to wait until time had passed, lest Felicity become pregnant at once—

seemed silly. It was unlikely that Felicity would become pregnant immediately, and if she did, what was the harm in that? Tongues might wag if a babe was born nine months after the wedding, but what did that matter to him? He would know that he was the father, and that was enough for him.

It was tempting to go to Felicity, and to avail himself of the rights that were his under law and custom. But still he hesitated, not wishing to shatter the fragile truce that they had built between them. He could not forget the sight of Felicity's pale, shocked face on the night he had rejected her. He had no guarantee that she would welcome his advances now. Indeed it would serve him right if she refused him.

And so he resolved to be patient, and to court his wife in earnest. This was not some dalliance. Felicity was his wife, and he had the rest of their lives to win her to him. But such thoughts were poor comfort in his empty bed.

On the fifth morning of their journey they left the home of Lord Lucan, and began their climb over the Caran Mountains. His heart quickened, for he knew that on the other side of that ridge lay the county of Kerry. From here they could reach Kilgarvan lands, if they took advantage of the long twilight for which Kerry was famed in the summer.

But the road that led through Connor's Gap was worse than he had expected. It was a mere donkey track at the best of times, but the recent storm had washed out sections and felled trees, forcing them to dismount and lead the horses around the obstacles. Each delay chafed at his nerves, but Felicity accepted them with equanimity. Then again, it was not her home that lay in the valley on the other side of the mountain range.

Of course he had no one to blame but himself. The difficulty of this route was the very reason that most travelers came by river and approached Kilgarvan from the west rather than make the mountain crossing. He had chosen this route hoping to discourage Felicity. Instead it was he who was discouraged.

The road wound up the mountainside in seemingly endless loops. At midmorning they paused, and only by looking back could he see how far they had come. Felicity stretched, her hands kneading her back as if she was sore and tired. He sympathized with her. His own calves ached in remembrance of the climb they had just made, while his thighs and backside protested the long hours on horseback.

He consulted his watch, and then looked carefully at what he could see of the trail ahead. If they pushed hard, and the road was no worse than it had been, they could make the summit by noon. From there it was still a dozen miles to Glenmore, but it would be downhill.

"This morning was slow going, but if we press hard and if luck is with us, we'll be in Glenmore by nightfall," he said aloud.

Leading the gray horse over to where Felicity stood, he handed her the reins, then cupped his hands together to help her mount. She weighed hardly more than a feather, and he tossed her into the saddle, where she settled with only a faint grimace to show the discomfort she felt.

"Then we must pray that our luck holds," Felicity replied. She did not want to know what her husband meant by pressing hard. In these last days she had begun to suspect that Kilgarvan could have taught Wellington's troops a thing or two about forced

marches. These last days of travel had been far more
grueling than she had expected.

But she wouldn't have exchanged places with anyone in the world. Since leaving Cork, Kilgarvan had
seemed to thaw, treating her with kindness and courtesy. Just as she had hoped, the journey had brought
them closer together, enabling them to resume their
old friendship. Not that she fooled herself into thinking that all was forgiven and forgotten. It was rather
that Kilgarvan seemed determined to make the best
of things, and she would do all she could to encourage him. And so she would journey on without word
of complaint, because she could see how much he
longed to return to his home.

And if her husband's newfound tolerance was not
enough to please her, there was also the Irish countryside, which had a wild beauty that delighted the eye
and spoke to her heart. Each day brought new wonders. The road led them by peaceful farms, through
wooded glens and along verdant hills dotted with
placidly grazing sheep. Gradually they had left the
lowlands behind, until they began the ascent of the
mountains.

The mountains were a forbidding sight, where
green grass and shrubs clung precariously to the
rock-studded hillsides. A narrow switchback path
wound up the side of the nearest of the mountains,
then disappeared into a gap between two peaks.

They reached the gap shortly after noon. Kilgarvan, who had been riding ahead due to the narrow-
ness of the trail, now stopped his horse. She rode up
alongside him.

She was about to remark on the trail, but the words
froze in her throat as she caught sight of his face.
Kilgarvan stared fiercely at the land below, with a look

of raw hunger and love. She felt a strange ache in her heart as she realized that no man had ever looked at her with such single-minded devotion.

Kilgarvan gazed below for what seemed an eternity. She followed his gaze, trying to fathom the source of his inspiration.

Below them, the hillside sloped in gentle folds down into a lush green valley. In the center of the valley was the silvery sheen of a lake. At the foot of the lake there appeared to be a small village or town, while along the far shore there were woods and what appeared to be a ruin of some sort. The land appeared lush and fertile, delighting the eye with all the myriad shades of green.

It was one of the most beautiful places she had ever seen. And yet that alone did not explain her husband's fascination.

"Is that Kilgarvan?" she asked, when she could endure his silence no longer.

Kilgarvan gave a start as he seemed to recall her presence.

"Yes. Or rather, it used to be. Once all this was Kilgarvan land," he said, gesturing with his free hand to indicate the valley. "But my ancestors paid a heavy price for their part in the rebellion of 1641. They lost most of the east end of the valley, and the lands that they had held in Kerry. Still, we were able to keep the best of the lot. Once we descend the hill, we will be on Kilgarvan land, and the town you see at the foot of the lake, that is Glenmore. My home."

She squinted, but could not make out any details.

"Come now. We may have to ride in the twilight, but we will spend this night under my own roof," he promised.

His home. His roof. His, and not hers or theirs.

Angry words leaped to her tongue, but she bit them back. No doubt it was just force of habit that had formed his words, rather than a deliberate attempt to exclude her.

Still, she could not help wondering what type of welcome awaited her at Glenmore. Would Kilgarvan's people treat her with the warmth and courtesy she had experienced during this journey? Or would they follow her husband's lead and treat her with the same cold disdain Kilgarvan had shown in the first days of their marriage?

She would have to wait to find out. As they left the gap, the path wound to the right. Past the first switchback she glimpsed a small cluster of cabins nestled in a fold of the hillside. As they drew nearer she could see that trestle tables had been set up outside of the largest cabin, and a crowd of villagers milled around outside.

Heads began to turn in their direction, and then she saw a small boy dash into one of the cabins. He came out a moment later, followed by a man moving at a more sedate speed.

Kilgarvan drew his horse to a stop. The man who approached was middle-aged, his dark hair streaked with gray, and his complexion reddened by endless seasons of work in the outdoors. He was better dressed than most peasants she had seen on the journey, his coat and trousers of dark blue, with a bright waistcoat.

The farmer hailed Kilgarvan in Gaelic. Her husband replied in the same tongue. Then the farmer looked over at her, and since she knew no Gaelic, she smiled instead.

"This is my wife, Lady Kilgarvan," her husband

said. "Felicity, this is Thomas Connolly, who farms the lands hereabout."

The farmer swept his hat from his head and made a quick bow. "God bless your ladyship," he said. "And it is begging your pardon, I am, for not having known you had no word of the Gaelic. Sure and it is the excitement of the day that has driven every thought from this old head of mine."

"I thank you for your blessing," Felicity replied.

The farmer surveyed her, then smiled, seeming pleased at what he saw. Then he turned back to Kilgarvan. "I must beg Shamus O'Sullivan's pardon when next I see him. Sure and didn't he tell me that you were bringing your countess by the old Cork road? And I says to him that you would have better sense, but here you are, showing me wrong, and now I owe that rascal Shamus a drink."

His voice was soft, and there was a twinkle in his eye as the farmer teased her husband.

"The old Cork road?" she asked pointedly.

Her husband had the grace to look discomfited. "It is the most direct route," he said.

"But not the easiest, I'll wager." She had long suspected as much, but it was pleasant to have her suspicions confirmed.

Thomas Connolly broke in. "I was just after telling your husband that my Nora is getting married today. And it would be the greatest honor to me and mine if you were to stay for the wedding."

"I thank you, but—" she started to say. She gladly would have stayed, but knew how anxious Kilgarvan was to see his home.

"It would be our honor to be your guests," her husband interrupted.

Thomas Connolly beamed and rubbed his hands

together. "Grand, grand," he declared. "My Nora
will be that proud when I tell her. Just follow me, and
I'll have one of my lazy sons see to your horses."

He went on ahead, and Felicity and Kilgarvan followed behind.

As soon as the farmer was out of earshot, she
turned to Kilgarvan. She said nothing, but raised one
eyebrow.

"It would shame them if we refused," he explained. "It would be seen as an insult to their hospitality. And besides, it is only a day. Arlyn Court will
still be there tomorrow."

She could only imagine how much that admission
had cost him. He had spoken of nothing these last
days save his need to be home, and now he was turning aside to satisfy the pride of a mere farmer. She
wished suddenly that they were not on horseback, for
she longed to take his hand in hers, and to let him
know how much she approved of his decision. It reminded her of the act of charity that had first brought
him to her attention.

They turned into the yard of the cottage, and there
was no time to talk privately as two young boys ran
up and held their horses as they dismounted. Kilgarvan was hailed by several of the men present, and
they were soon separated as Mrs. Connolly came to
urge Felicity to come inside to freshen up.

The cabin was dark after the bright sunshine outdoors, and Felicity stood for a moment in the doorway, blinking her eyes as she struggled to see in the
dim light.

The room they had entered was obviously the main
living room of the house. On the left was a fireplace,
where a kettle simmered above a low fire. Next to the
hearth were shelves holding small baskets and jars of

provisions. The floor was dirt, but swept clean, and small indentations showed where a table and chairs no doubt normally rested.

In the corner a ladder led up, presumably to a loft. The right wall held a curtained-off opening, and what appeared to be a bedroom.

"Nora, come quick," Mrs. Connolly called. " 'Tis her ladyship herself, come to wish you merry on your wedding day."

A hand drew the curtain aside and Nora appeared. She was a young woman, with dark eyes and curly brown hair that streamed down her back. Her cheeks were dusted with freckles, and dimpled as she smiled.

"You are welcome to this house," she said. "And it is good luck indeed to have a stranger at the wedding."

"Thank you," Felicity said. "And I wish you joy on your wedding day."

Just then there was a hiss, and a pot began to boil over. "Saints have mercy, if it is not one thing it is another," Mrs. Connolly exclaimed, hurrying over to remove the kettle from the fire. "Begging your pardon, your ladyship, but I must be taking this outside to cool. Nora, take her into the bedroom and let her tidy herself up."

So saying, Mrs. Connolly carried the kettle outside.

"I do not want to be any trouble," Felicity said.

"Oh, no, it is no trouble at all. You are our guest, and everyone will understand. And besides," she said, her brown eyes dancing, "Brian has waited two years for me already. Another hour will not hurt him a bit."

Felicity digested this bit of information as she followed Nora into the bedroom. She wondered what

it was like to be so sure of your love that you were
willing to wait two years for him.

A boy brought in her saddlebags, and with Nora's
help Felicity washed her hands and face, and combed
her hair into a respectable chignon. She thought for
a moment about changing from her riding habit into
the one good dress she had, but then decided against
it. She did not want to outshine Nora on her wedding
day.

Not that Nora need be concerned. The cheerful
happiness that bubbled up from her more than com-
pensated for the simplicity of her costume. And the
embroidered blue wool skirt and linen blouse were
surely new for this special day.

Felicity would cheerfully have given Nora a present
of one of her gowns, but Nora was several inches
shorter and decidedly plumper around the waist.
And even if they were of a size, she would not want
to risk giving offense, either to Nora or to whomever
had so lovingly embroidered the clothes for this day.

After pinning her hair up, Felicity checked her appearance in the tiny mirror that hung from the wall.
She would have to do, she thought, then gathered
up her comb and brush and placed them in her case.
As she placed them back in her saddlebag, her hand
encountered the familiar shape of her keepsake box.
She had carried it with her all this time, refusing to
leave it behind. Gowns, shawls, shoes and even jewelry had been left behind to be conveyed by wagon.
But she would not be parted from her keepsakes.

Suddenly she was glad that she had insisted on
bringing this box with her, despite Kilgarvan's grum-
blings on how awkward it was to pack. Opening the
box, she carefully moved aside the shells till the glit-
ter of gems revealed what she sought. She removed

the two combs and then closed the box, replacing it firmly in her luggage.

She held the combs in her hand for a moment, remembering how delighted she had been when Senhora Almadillo had presented them to her. Smaller than the elaborate combs worn by the women of the Portuguese court, they were perfect for the young lady she had been. Her first grown-up jewelry, the senhora had declared, and young Felicity had worshiped the elegant woman who had given her such a wonderful gift.

And now it was time to pass these on to another. Nora was peering out the window, no doubt hoping to catch a glimpse of her Brian.

"Nora," Felicity said, coming to stand behind her. "You will see your Brian soon enough."

Nora laughed. "And when he is my own, no doubt I will soon be wishful to see the backside of him," she said.

"Here, let me help you with your hair," Felicity said. She turned Nora so her back was to the mirror, and then quickly tucked a comb in on each side, just above the ear.

"There," she said.

Nora turned to see her reflection in the mirror. "Oh, my," she murmured. "Oh, my."

Indeed the combs looked very elegant, and Felicity felt quite pleased with herself for having thought of them.

"They are so beautiful. I promise to take good care of them, and to give them back to you right after."

"They are yours. A gift for your wedding day," Felicity said. "And for your kindness in inviting Lord Kilgarvan and me to share in it."

"But I couldn't. I can't," Nora babbled in confu-

sion, reaching up to touch one of the magnificent
objects, then turning to look at Felicity. "I mean, I
shouldn't, should I?"

"Of course you can," Felicity said. "They are a gift
from me to you. And someday you can give them to
your daughter on her wedding day."

"God will bless you for your kindness," Nora said.

"Come now. Brian is waiting for us," Felicity said,
uncomfortable with such expressions of gratitude.

They went outside into the sunlight together.

Eleven

The wedding was officiated by Father Harrington, who had made the long trip from Glenmore on foot. At least fifty people were present to witness the vows, for the Connollys and their neighbors had been joined by friends and relations from the east side of the valley. During the ceremony Kilgarvan and Felicity stood in the back, as befitted their status as guests at the Catholic ceremony. But as soon as the vows were over, Kilgarvan had been the first man to kiss the bride, to wish her luck in her new life.

During the feasting Kilgarvan and Felicity had been given a spot of honor, squeezed together on a bench at the head of the table, next to the newlyweds and Father Harrington. There were ham roasts, mutton pies and salted herring, not to mention the ubiquitous potatoes. Felicity had gamely tried each new dish, seeming to enjoy herself thoroughly. Kilgarvan had dug in as well, but his enjoyment of the simple country cooking was tempered by the feeling of Felicity's body pressed tightly against his side.

The Connollys were more prosperous than most of their neighbors, and it showed in the lavish feast they had provided for their daughter. There was food and drink in abundance, and everyone there ate their fill and more. Then one man brought out his pipes, and another his fiddle, and the company rose from their seats, eager to begin the dancing.

Felicity was swept away by the womenfolk, and Kilgarvan allowed himself to be parted from her. He glanced her way from time to time, but she seemed to be enjoying herself. Luckily the Connollys were a progressive family, and most of them spoke English, so there was no worry there.

The fiddler struck up a reel, and the piper joined in. Brian seized a laughing Nora from a circle of her friends and dragged her to the open space just beyond the tables. There the two began to dance and were swiftly joined by other young couples.

Kilgarvan accepted a glass of native whiskey and stood with the older men under the shade of an oak tree, watching the dancing and listening to their conversation. After they complimented Thomas Connolly on his hospitality, and compared this wedding to other weddings they had attended in the past, the conversation soon turned to the usual topics: the weather, their cattle, the market for butter, and the prospects for the potato and oat crops.

At Kilgarvan's request they shared news of Glenmore, and he learned that several of the young men had left for England only this past week, seeking employment as seasonal harvesters. Matthew Sweeney, who had emigrated to America five years before, had finally sent passage money so his wife and children could join him. The Hanlons and the Murphys were quarreling again, this time over the ownership of a young bull. Blows had been exchanged, but no blood had been shed, and the parties had agreed to wait for the earl to return to judge the matter.

Kilgarvan was content to listen, and to soak up the

news of home. He realized what a rare privilege it
was that these men would share the concerns of their
lives with him, treating him with respect but without
the false deference that they would give an English-
man.

Thomas Connolly rejoined them, carrying a jug
and making sure to refill everyone's glass. "And did
his lordship tell you that he brought his new bride
by way of the old Cork road?"

There was a general exclamation of disbelief, and
heads turned in his direction. Kilgarvan nodded to
confirm the truth of the statement, and then held
his composure as the men offered their suggestions
on how he could have more pleasantly spent his wedding journey.

"Now, now, there is no need for that talk," Thomas
Connolly said firmly. "Herself is a fine lady, and I
know that these blackguards mean no disrespect."

"A fine lady, indeed," Tim Connolly offered.

"A treasure, and a grace to your noble house," old
Ned Devine added. "Here's a health to you and to
your good wife, and our best wishes for your happiness."

"To your happiness," the men echoed, raising
their glasses and taking a drink.

Kilgarvan drank as well. "My thanks," he said. His
eyes swept the crowd, but Felicity was no longer standing talking with Mrs. Connolly. At last he found her
amid the dancers. Sean Connolly, Nora's eldest
brother, was laughing broadly as he attempted to
guide Felicity through the steps of a country dance.

"Your wife has the look of a fine woman. A real
lady. And generous too," Thomas Connolly said, with
the hint of a question in his voice.

Kilgarvan knew the hidden meaning behind his

host's words. No doubt all present knew that he had gone to London in search of a well-dowered wife. And yet his appearance with Felicity, traveling the roughest of roads, with neither baggage cart nor servant, was hardly likely to inspire confidence that he had succeeded. But courtesy was inbred in these people. If he and Felicity had been mere beggars, they still would have been welcomed to the celebrations. And he knew that if he chose to ignore the unspoken question that this would be the end of the matter, and they would respect his rights to keep his own counsel.

But there was no need for such. He had intended to tell the people of Glenmore first, but though these men were not his tenants, there were still remnants of the ancient allegiance. Those who eked out a precarious living on the slopes of the east valley were the friends and relations of Kilgarvan's own tenants. They, too, had suffered when Kilgarvan's father could no longer afford to employ servants and laborers, and when he had raised rents on his own lands, the surrounding rents had been raised as well.

"I am a lucky man," Kilgarvan said. "And my good fortune will be shared. There will be work for those that want it. Beginning with setting right the old Cork road."

"God bless you," old Ned Devine said in a quavering voice.

The desperate hope in these men's eyes was suddenly too much for him to bear. Kilgarvan excused himself and sought out his wife.

Weaving his way among the dancers, he tapped Sean Connolly on the shoulder. "This woman is already taken," he said.

Sean relinquished his place with a mock mournful sigh, and a pledge to Felicity of eternal devotion.

Felicity's face was flushed with exertion, and her eyes sparkled up at Kilgarvan. "Thank you for rescuing me," she said. "I could scarce catch my breath. Do these dances never end?"

"Not as long as the sunlight holds, and the musicians are kept well supplied with drink," he answered. He escorted her to the sidelines, since that was her wish, repressing a pang of disappointment. He would not have minded an excuse to hold Felicity in his arms.

Felicity sat down on one of the benches and cheerfully accepted his offer to fetch her a glass of water. He returned, handing her the glass and sitting down beside her.

"They make a lovely couple," she said.

"Yes," he agreed. While it was true that Brian Sullivan would win no medals for handsomeness, it was plain to see that the young man was head over heels in love with his new bride, and it was just as clear that Nora returned his affection in full measure. There was an almost visible glow of happiness around the new couple, which lent a cheerful energy to the celebration. This was how a wedding should be, and he pushed aside memories of their own wedding day.

"I take it Nora has you to thank for the combs in her hair," he observed. "I wonder if she would dance the jig quite so vigorously if she knew she had a year's rent adorning those brown locks."

"Every bride deserves to feel beautiful on her wedding day," Felicity said.

Her words were reflective, but nonetheless he felt a stab of guilt. He knew full well that Felicity had felt anything but cherished and beautiful on her wedding

day. They had gone through the ceremony with all
the warmth of two strangers executing a business contract. And then, on that one night when she should
have felt special, he had allowed his pride and anger
to rule him. He had rejected his wife, refusing to
share her bed.

He had been stupid and blind, and he knew he
had wounded Felicity deeply. But instead of responding with bitterness she had treated him with forbearance, in her own stubborn, headstrong way.

He would give anything to be able to take back
those words. To be able to start afresh, and to treat
his wife with the courtesy she deserved.

A cheer arose from the guests.

"What is happening?" Felicity asked, looking over
to the dance floor.

He rose and saw that a half dozen young lads had
surrounded Nora and Brian, and with whoops of encouragement were escorting the young couple away
from the celebration.

"It is time for Nora and Brian to take their leave,"
he said. "The boys will escort them to the cabin
where they will live, and post a guard to see that no
one disturbs the newlyweds. Save themselves, of
course."

"Of course."

Twilight was falling, and the guests with long walks
ahead of them had begun to take their leave. Soon
it would be time for Felicity and Kilgarvan to retire
for the night. But for now, the musicians were still
playing, and Kilgarvan gave in to the desire that had
tempted him all afternoon.

Taking Felicity's hand in his, he said, "My lady, may
I have the honor of this dance?"

The dancers gave way to them as he led her to the

center of the grassy square that served as the dance floor. The musicians finished the hornpipe with a flourish, and then stood awaiting the next request. He was conscious that all eyes were on them. Even the children had ceased weaving in and out among the guests in their interminable game of tag, and stood quietly, trying to fathom what had caused this interruption.

Kilgarvan took Felicity's hand in his own, and then placed his other on the small of her back. "A slow reel, if you please." Sean Connolly had been content to partner Felicity in a country set, but Kilgarvan had something quite different in mind.

The fiddler nodded, and as the musicians began to play, Kilgarvan led Felicity in the steps of a waltz. There were a few false steps as they adjusted themselves to the new rhythm, but within moments they were moving as one.

He drew her closer to him, in a manner that would have been quite scandalous in London, but allowed him to enjoy the feel of her in his arms. He marveled at her slender form, which gave no hint of her inner core of steel.

From the corner of his eye he could see that other couples had joined in, but he paid them no heed. He had eyes only for Felicity.

"I have wanted to do this all day," he said, feeling a grin stretch across his face.

Felicity laughed. "And here I thought you had left your dancing days behind in England."

England. It seemed so far away and long ago, as if he had met Felicity there in another life. Or perhaps the man he had been in London had been a different man indeed. It was hard to recall how desperate he had been, knowing that he would lose his birthright unless he won the favor of an heiress. Any heiress. If he had not met Felicity, he might even now be married to Miss Sawyer, or, worse yet, forced to watch helplessly as everything he owned was taken from him.

Looking down at Felicity's bent head, he realized how incredibly lucky he had been to find her. Or, rather, how lucky it had been that she had found him. Using the cover of the dance, he pulled her close to him. "Thank you," he whispered in her ear.

"For what?"

"For everything," he answered.

The endless summer twilight began to wane, until only a handful of the Connollys' closest neighbors remained. The tables and benches had long since been returned to their owners, and the musicians had packed up their instruments while families collected small children who had exhausted themselves into slumber. A few courting couples remained, strolling hand in hand in the meadow, exchanging confidences before they parted.

"The Connollys have offered us their hospitality for the evening, and I think it is time we retire," he said.

"Very well," Felicity agreed. "Although I can't remember a time when I have enjoyed myself more."

They bade good night to the Connollys, Felicity complimenting them again on the glorious celebration. Then he took Felicity by the hand and led her to the Connollys' cabin.

A lantern had been lit and placed on the table inside, illuminating the center of the room but casting dark shadows in the corners. Toward the right the curtain that separated the main room from the bedroom had been tucked to one side, and he could see the faint glow of rushlights on the dresser within.

Felicity followed him in and then stopped. "There is no one here," she said.

"The Connollys have offered us their cabin for the night," he explained.

Felicity released his hand and took a few steps inside. Her eyes drifted to the bedroom, and then she turned back to face him. "But this is their home. And they have been so kind to us. Surely we cannot put them out of their own house on the day of their own daughter's wedding?"

He advanced toward her slowly. "On the contrary. This is why we must accept. It would be a slur upon their hospitality to do otherwise."

"But—"

"In Ireland the guest is always given the best of everything. There can be no greater praise than to call someone generous, and no greater insult than to refer to someone as stingy and inhospitable. Thomas Connolly and his family will sleep well tonight at his brother's house across the road, pleased to know that you have accepted their hospitality."

Felicity nodded, but she began to worry her lower lip, as if something was preying on her mind. "I appreciate their generosity," she began. "But there is only the one bed."

She turned her head as she said those words. He could not be sure in the dim lantern light, but he thought he saw a blush upon her cheeks.

He closed the distance between them, taking her hands in his. "There is always the loft, where Nora and her brothers make their beds. If you wish, I will sleep there tonight. But I would very much like to spend the night with you."

He held his breath, and tried to still the rapid beating of his heart as he waited for her answer. Eons seemed to tick by, and he braced himself for disappointment.

Then she lifted her head and looked him directly in the eyes. "Yes," she said, her voice trembling only a little. "I would like that very much."

He released his breath in a rush as her answer sank in. Releasing her hands, he cupped his hands around her face, his eyes drinking in the sight of her so he could remember this moment for the rest of his life. He could see anticipation mingled with trepidation in her eyes, and he felt a sudden rush of tenderness.

He would be gentle with her, he vowed to himself. He would make up to her all the hurt he had caused her, and teach her the joys of marriage as he should have done weeks ago.

He bent his head down and brushed her lips with his own. Her soft lips pressed against his own with sweet innocence, and one of her hands reached up to caress his neck. It took all his iron control to keep from deepening the kiss. There would be time for that later, he promised himself. But for now, gentleness and patience were required.

Reluctantly he ended the kiss and raised his head. The results were all he could have wished for. Felicity's face was flushed, and her lips swollen. She looked at him with amazement, and the beginnings of a hunger for more.

"Oh, my," she said.

Her inarticulateness was the greatest compliment he had ever received.

"I promise you there are even more delights to be

discovered," he said, reaching up to loosen the pins that held her hair in place. Her auburn hair cascaded down her back, and he ran his hands through its silky length, as he had longed to do for so many days.

"Come," he said, taking her hand in his and leading her into the bedroom.

Twelve

When Felicity awoke the next morning, she was alone. But Kilgarvan had not been gone long, for she could see the impression of his head on the pillow, and, pressing her hand to the blanket, could feel the warmth from where he had lain beside her. She smiled to herself as she remembered their lovemaking the night before. Their kiss had only hinted at the pleasures she had discovered in Kilgarvan's arms. Never had she imagined it possible to feel such delight. And when their bodies had joined, she had felt as if their souls had briefly touched as well.

She hoped that she had pleased him as well as he had pleasured her.

She wondered why so many women had described the marriage act as unpleasant or tedious, and then realized it must be the fault of their husbands. The visage of Sir Percy Lambeth sprang to her mind, and with it the knowledge that if she had not seen Kilgarvan that night at the theater, she might very well have married Sir Percy, or another gentleman very much like him. And yet she could not imagine herself sharing such intimacies with Sir Percy, or indeed with anyone else except Kilgarvan.

She heard the sound of a door, and then a woman's voice from the next room called, "Good morning."

"Good morning," she heard Kilgarvan reply.

Heavens! The Connollys had returned, and she was still lying abed. What would they think? She threw back the covers, preparing to rise, only to discover that she was completely nude. Hastily she wrapped the quilt around her, certain she was blushing from head to toe. Frantically she glanced around the room, all too conscious that the only thing that separated her from those chattering in the kitchen was a mere length of cloth that served as the door.

Rising from the bed she saw clothing laid out on a chair, and on the small chest of drawers was a basin, a pitcher of water and a linen washcloth. She blessed Kilgarvan for his thoughtfulness, for she knew that these had not been there the night before.

She poured the water into the basin slowly, trying to avoid making any sound that would announce her presence. As she washed herself, she heard someone moving around the kitchen, and then the unmistakable sounds of cracking eggs and sizzling meat. Soon enticing odors were drifting into the bedroom.

Felicity donned her blue riding habit. The hem had become frayed during the trip, but soon it would not matter. For this day they would reach her new home, and her traveling would be over.

She pulled on her half boots, then checked her appearance one last time in the mirror. Surely there ought to be some sign that she had become a woman? Some outward sign that she had replaced her innocence with knowledge of desire? And yet try as she could, she could see no alteration in her appearance. She felt like a new person, but if the mirror were to be trusted, she looked the same as she always had.

"Good morning," Felicity said, as she pushed aside the curtain and entered the kitchen.

"And a fine morning to you," Mrs. Connolly said, turning from the fireplace. "Just sit yourself down, and I will have breakfast ready before you know it."

Felicity glanced over to the table, where Kilgarvan was seated. She briefly caught his eye and then looked away in confusion. How was one supposed to behave toward one's husband, after the intimacies they had shared?

Carefully she sat down across from him.

"I trust you slept well?" he asked

"Yes," she replied, although indeed there had been very little sleep that occurred last night.

She looked at the table and realized it was set for two. "Will not Mr. Connolly join us?" she asked.

The question had been addressed to Kilgarvan, but it was Mrs. Connolly who replied. "Ah, that one," she said. "Himself and our sons were awake hours ago. My sister Mary Kate made a fine breakfast for us all, and now they are up on the meadows, tending to the cattle."

"You should not have let me sleep so late," Felicity said.

Kilgarvan gave a slow smile, full of hidden meaning. "You seemed tired, after the . . . the excitement of yesterday," he said smoothly. "I saw no harm in letting you sleep late this morning. From here it is an easy journey to Glenmore, and we will be there by afternoon."

Mrs. Connolly wrapped her apron around the handle of a frying pan, and then lifted it from the fire. Bringing the pan over to the table, she loaded their plates with a generous portion of eggs, bacon and fried potatoes, and then brought over a loaf of bread, cut into thick slices and spread with butter.

Felicity fell to her meal with a ravenous hunger that she had not suspected till the food was laid in front of her.

Mrs. O'Connell refused to join them, but instead kept up a steady stream of conversation as she busied herself around the kitchen. Felicity was grateful for her presence, for the cheerful chatter distracted her from any lingering awkwardness between her and Kilgarvan.

"And it's right glad I was to hear that the men would be hired on for fixing the road. Sure and there will be many a man who will be grateful for honest work," Mrs. O'Connell remarked.

Kilgarvan nodded, but instead of replying took a sip of his tea.

After breakfast they bade farewell to Mrs. O'Connell, thanking her again for her hospitality. Then they mounted their horses and began the journey down into the valley.

As soon as they were alone, Kilgarvan turned to Felicity. "I hope it is not too uncomfortable for you to ride?"

"Oh! No," she said, blushing as she realized his meaning. In truth she was a bit sore, but it was only a short distance to Glenmore.

"Good. I was afraid we had been a trifle enthusiastic last night," he said with a wicked grin.

She felt the heat in her face, and wondered if she would ever feel comfortable discussing such a matter with her husband. Desperately she sought to change the subject. "Mrs. O'Connell mentioned something about fixing a road? And your offering employment to the men hereabouts?"

"Surely after this last week, even you can see that the Cork road needs to be repaired. At least from here to Drisheen," he said.

"Of course. But why should we pay for its upkeep?" she asked, stressing the word *we*. "You don't even own the property that it runs along. Should you not apply to the government to repair the roads?"

His words were cold and clipped as he replied. "The government cares naught for a minor road in the uncivilized south. They will not pay a farthing for its upkeep. The condition of the road does not matter to them. But it does to me, and to the farmers of Kilgarvan. Nowadays they must take their butter and cattle to market in Nedeen, or even farther to Killarney. The journey is long, and the prices there are only half of what they could command in the great market at Cork. If we fix the road, the farmers can get a fair price for their goods. They will prosper, as will we. The investment in the road will pay for itself in a few years."

"You seem to have thought this out very well," she said, seeing the logic in his words.

"It was no mere whim when I offered the work yesterday," he said.

"I was not questioning your judgment," she said. "Merely the timing of your announcement. You had days to share your plans with me, and yet I hear of this only today. If Mrs. Connolly had not spoken, when were you going to inform me?"

There was a long pause. "I did not mean to exclude you," Kilgarvan said. "I am not used to sharing my counsel with anyone. I will promise to do better."

"Thank you," she said. There was a moment's pause, and then when it became clear that Kilgarvan was not going to speak, she prompted him with, "And are there any other projects I should be informed of?"

"My intentions are not yet fixed," Kilgarvan replied. "There are various schemes that have been long considered, but I could not decide on any till I knew how much capital would be available to implement them."

She translated the sentence in her head, and realized he meant that his plans had been dependent on his obtaining a wife, and the size of her dowry. She nodded, encouraging him to go on.

"I have sent for a friend of mine, to ask his help in starting a school for the children," he began. "And written to several factory owners, to see about the possibility of starting a factory that would give year-round employment. Then there is the great house to set to rights, and decisions to be made on whether to repair the tenants' cabins or simply tear them down and build anew. There were once weirs on the lake, to provide fish, and they could be built again. And of course the cattle herds are in a poor state, the best bulls having been sold off long ago. My agent, Dennis O'Connor, suggested sending to Killarney to purchase a fine bull, which could be set to stud. And then—"

His face was animated, and he gestured enthusiastically as he began to describe the various schemes he had devised. Felicity admired his passion, but feared that he was letting his enthusiasm override his good sense. She did not see how one man could implement even half the schemes he proposed, and her dowry, while sizable, was not infinite.

He seemed to sense her reservations, for he suddenly paused in his description of how a model town could be designed. "You must think me foolish," he said.

"No," she said slowly. "But—"

"But these things cannot be done overnight," he said, as if he could read her mind. "It will take time, and patience, to do all I hope for. Still, it does no harm to have great dreams, even if the beginnings must be small."

The tension left her as she realized her fears had been foolish. She must remember to trust her husband's judgment, as he would learn to trust hers. They were partners in this venture, after all. His was the land, and hers was the money that would make it prosper. And together they would see those dreams come to fruition.

The strained atmosphere evaporated, and they spoke easily of the fine wedding, and the people she had met there. They made good progress, and the lake, which had appeared as a silver ribbon from the mountaintop, grew steadily larger, the sun sparkling off its dark waters. From time to time he pointed out sights to her. A stone cairn that marked the resting place of an ancient hero. The crumbling remains of cabins, deserted when their inhabitants could no longer pay the rent.

Strangely there was no joy in his face when he pointed out the ancient oak tree that marked the border of Kilgarvan land. Given his impatience to reach home, she had expected him to rejoice, but instead he grew quiet, and his face became still and impenetrable.

"Is there something wrong?" she asked.

"No," he replied quickly, but she did not believe him. There was tension in the set of his shoulders, and his expression was grim.

She looked ahead, but could not see what had caused his sudden reserve. The road had leveled out as they reached the floor of the valley. Up ahead to the right lay the glistening waters of the lake. Not far from the lake there were a group of men laboring in a muddy field. They appeared to be making bricks, but when she asked Kilgarvan, she was informed that the men were cutting turf. So that was where the peat bricks that the Irish burned in their fires came from. She had never seen such a thing before, and promised herself she would return for a closer look someday soon.

"Remember that Glenmore has fallen on hard times," he said, his remarks addressed to the road before them, rather than his looking her in the eye.

"Of course," she said.

As they rounded the southern end of the lake, she saw a cabin standing in a field. One wall of the cabin was crumbling, the front door was missing entirely and the straw thatch roof was a dull brown, a sure sign of disrepair. At first she thought it another abandoned residence, but as they drew closer she saw smoke coming from the chimney, and a few listless chickens scratching in the yard.

Next to the cabin was a small patch of potatoes. A woman and a girl were weeding the field, but at the sound of the horses they looked up, and they both bobbed a curtsy as the woman called out a greeting in Gaelic.

Kilgarvan merely nodded in acknowledgment. Felicity could not help noticing that both the woman and the child were barefoot, and the skirts they had looped up for working were little better than rags.

No doubt some tragedy had overtaken this family, she told herself. But she could not contain her unease as they passed the next cottage, and another. Each was in as poor condition as the first.

Dogs barked, and children ran out from the cabins as they reached the village of Glenmore. *Village* was too grand a name for it. A miserable collection of perhaps two dozen cabins lined either side of the road. None of them deserved to be called anything other than hovels.

At the center of the village was a small green on which a pair of scrawny black cattle grazed. On one side of the green was a small chapel, and next to it was a two-story building of stone that might have been a store or an estate office once, but now sat idle. On the other side of the green was what appeared to be a blacksmith's shop, though the forge was unlit. There were a couple of other buildings whose purpose was not immediately apparent.

Past the green the road led up a small rise to where a great manor house stood. From here it appeared to be a grand establishment, and completely out of place when compared to the village.

Kilgarvan stopped his horse on the green and dismounted, and Felicity did the same. A crowd gathered around them, calling greetings in Gaelic. The villagers seemed pleased to see Kilgarvan. There were many interested glances in her direction, and Felicity forced herself to smile back at the friendly faces, trying desperately to hide her shock.

Never had she expected to see such misery. When Kilgarvan had told her his people were poor, she had imagined poverty as she had seen it in England, not this desperate privation. She had seen beggars walking the roads in England who appeared better clothed and fed than the residents of Glenmore.

Not that the people were starved. She had seen

starvation in India, and these people did not have that dreadful thinness or hollow, sunken gaze. But neither were they well fed, although observing the crowds she could see that while the adults were all lean and wiry, the children had rosy round cheeks and bright eyes.

A young man, better dressed than any she had seen so far, called out to Kilgarvan, and the crowd parted to let him make his way through.

He paused in front of them and made a bow that would have done credit in an English drawing room. "Welcome home, my lord," he said. Then he turned his attention to her. "A thousand welcomes to you, Lady Felicity. It is pleased we are to have you here."

"Thank you," Felicity said.

"Felicity, this is my agent, Dennis O'Connor," her husband said by way of introduction.

"I am pleased to meet you, Mr. O'Connor."

Kilgarvan turned away from her as a laborer asked him a question in Gaelic. In a moment Mr. O'Connor was called into the discussion.

Felicity looked around, feeling excluded. A young girl came up to her and shyly stroked the velvet embroidery on the sleeve of Felicity's riding habit. Then the girl tipped her head up and asked a question.

"I am sorry," Felicity said with a shake of her head. "I do not speak Gaelic."

She glanced around, but while the faces appeared friendly enough, no one came forward with an offer to translate. She could feel the smile on her face growing stiff, but did not know what else she could do.

Turning to her husband, she placed her hand on his sleeve. Kilgarvan turned and frowned as he recalled her presence.

"I must take Felicity up to the house," he informed Dennis O'Connor.

Dennis nodded. "You'll find everything that can be done has been done. Father Harrington told us you'd be arriving today, and my mother and sister are up there now."

"Good," Kilgarvan said.

He helped Felicity mount her horse, and then mounted his own. "I will meet you here in half an hour, and you can bring me up-to-date on how our plans are progressing," he told Dennis. Then, after a few farewell exchanges to the villagers, he and Felicity resumed their journey.

The end of her travels was within her grasp, yet she was no longer anxious for the journey to end. Glenmore had shocked her to her core, and she wondered what other surprises this land held for her.

Thirteen

Felicity had been horrified by her first sight of Glenmore. Kilgarvan had seen it in her face before she had time to don a polite social mask. But he could see the distress that lurked behind her gaze, and her shock upon discovering the true state of affairs. He had known that she would be dismayed by what she saw, but still he had felt a stab of betrayal as he witnessed her shock.

He saw Glenmore as it must appear through her eyes. Everywhere there were signs of dire poverty: the dilapidated cabins, the tattered rags his people wore, the lack of industry. Where once the hillsides had been dotted with cattle, now there were only a few straggly beasts remaining, the rest having been sold off long ago to make the rent.

Even the faces of the people were thinner than he remembered. He felt sick as he thought of the fine meals he had enjoyed in London, while his people were subsisting on potatoes and milk.

He had known his people were poor, but now he realized that they stood on the edge of a catastrophe. It would take little to push them over into disaster. A crop failure, a summer with too much or too little rain, a cattle sickness. Any one of these would finish these people off.

He cursed himself for his blindness. The decline had occurred gradually during his youth, and continued after his father's death. He had seen that his people were poor, but like his father he had seen not what was, but what he dreamed could be. It had taken his absence in London, and then his return, to open his eyes to the plight of his people. And now he saw them as his new wife must, and he felt ashamed. No accusation that his wife could hurl at him could wound him as much as his own reproaches.

This is not my fault, he had wanted to cry out, but his pride held him frozen in silence. He would not explain to her. Coming on this trip had been her idea. He had warned her that Glenmore was not fit for civilized company, and that she would be better off waiting until he could set things right before making a visit. But, damn her stubbornness, Felicity had insisted on making the journey, and upon her own head be it if she did not like what she had found.

Politeness held her tongue while they were in company, but as soon as they were alone, he knew she would begin to question him. And he could not bear it. So he had bundled her quickly up to the main house, leaving her to the care of Dennis's mother and sister, both of whom spoke fair English. She had asked to come with him, but he had refused, telling her that she would be better served inspecting the house and getting settled.

He thought for a moment that she would refuse his command, but then she acceded. Or rather, it was not that she obeyed his wish, but found her own reasons to do as he said. Felicity had her own streak of stubbornness, and he knew that if she had thought it best, she was more than capable of insisting on following him.

He needed time to think, so he left his horse at the stable and walked the mile back to the village. There he found Dennis O'Connor in quiet conversation with young Dan O'Sullivan, who was nephew to Thomas Connolly, their host from the previous day. As was the custom in Ireland, Thomas Connolly had rented a large property, and then in turn rented portions of this to his relations. The O'Sullivans were a large family, eleven children in all, with Dan being the eldest. While not as prosperous as their cousins, they did well, compared to their neighbors in Kilgarvan.

But there were seven sons in the O'Sullivan family, and the land could not support them all. Even if Thomas Connolly was willing to further divide the land he rented, he had five sons of his own to provide for. The O'Sullivans, like most in the valley, faced a hard choice. They could remain, trying to eke out a meager living on a tiny patch of ground, supplementing their farming with a few days labor here and there.

Or they could leave, seeking employment in England or emigrating to the Americas.

It was a brutally hard choice, for those who emigrated never returned, and were counted as dead to their family.

As he approached, the two ceased speaking and turned to greet him.

"Lord Kilgarvan," Dennis said, with a nod of his head.

Dan O'Sullivan pulled off his cap and clutched it to his chest. "Your lordship," he said, his voice cracking on the last word.

"Dan here was just after telling me that you were hiring men on to clear the road to Cork." There was not quite a question in his overseer's voice.

"Indeed," Kilgarvan replied.

"And what were you thinking? Did you simply want the road cleared and leveled? Or should we send to England for Mr. Macadam, and ask him to put in one of his fine new roads?"

This time the sarcasm in his tone was obvious. Young Dan flinched, but Kilgarvan was an earl, and made of sterner stuff. "A simple clearing should suffice," he said. "Once the worst of the rock slides are cleared, and the holes filled in, the road should be passable. A dozen men ought to be able to finish this before the harvest. You can start with Dan O'Sullivan here, and then find eleven stout helpers."

"I thank you, sir," Dan said, his young face beaming with pleasure. "And my mother thanks you, and my father as well. And a hundred thousand blessings upon you and your new wife—"

"Yes, yes," Kilgarvan said, before Dan could begin to recite the names of his ancestors, and to express his gratitude on their behalf. "Go home and tell your neighbors that we'll need five more men, and Dennis will pick half a dozen from the valley. Just one man from each family, and make sure they are fit for the work. It will be hard labor, but I will pay a shilling a day until it is done."

Dan expressed his thanks several more times before he was finally persuaded to leave.

"Come," Kilgarvan said to Dennis. "We will walk, and you can tell me what you have been up to these past weeks."

Dennis fell into step beside him. "I'm right glad that you are here," he said. "We'd been expecting you any day now this past fortnight. And you could have knocked me over with a feather when I heard you were bringing the new countess here. I thought you were to leave her in Dublin."

"I had not bargained on Lady Felicity's determination," Kilgarvan said. "She would not be left behind, and insisted on making the journey here."

"And so you took her by the Cork road, hoping to discourage her," Dennis said with a grin. "Seems she isn't the type to discourage easily."

"No. She has a will of iron."

Dennis thought this over a moment, then nodded. "I'd say you were well matched, being as stubborn as the devil yourself. All in all, I'd say you had got yourself a rare one. Fortune, beauty and character."

"Thank you," Kilgarvan said, but he did not wish to discuss his wife, not even with his oldest friend. Not while his feelings toward her were so confused.

"Has John Bradshaw arrived?" he asked, changing the subject.

"Not yet, but he sent a letter ahead, and should be here any day."

As they left the village, they followed the road as it curved west along the lake, and Dennis began pointing out various projects that had been started.

A section of the common meadow had been cleared and fenced in, awaiting the bull that Dennis had purchased in Nedeen. Equipment had been ordered from Killarney, including iron plows for the farmers, and saws and hammers for the laborers.

"Myself and Jerry O'Connell have gone round to all the cabins and made a list of repairs that are needed. Some need doing right away; others can wait for a bit. And some of the cabins are in such miserable shape that it might be cheaper to tear them

down and build anew. But we did not start the work,
waiting for you to decide what needed to be done
first."

It was hard to believe any of the cabins could be
salvaged, but Jerry O'Connell had been a master
builder, and if he said so, it must be true.

"I will see Jerry O'Connell tomorrow, and we three
can go over the lists," Kilgarvan promised. "As for
the rest, once John Bradshaw arrives, he can start
with the surveying."

"It is just a fortnight till the rent is due. Are you
still of a mind to forgive the half-year's rent?" Dennis
asked.

"It seems the decent thing to do."

Dennis shook his head. "You forgive the rent and
they'll spend it on poteen at the fair, and they'll be
no better off than before. No, if you are of a mind
to be charitable, you should collect the rent and use
the money to build a fishing weir that all can work
in common."

There was sense in Dennis's words, and an understanding of his own people. While some might indeed save the money, or spend it on the necessities
such as food or clothing, there were those who were
unaccustomed to having any spare coin at all. The
coins would slip through their fingers, and they
would spend the next half year wondering where
their good fortune had gone.

"Very well," Kilgarvan said. "Though I doubt if
half of them will have the full rent."

"And you'll have to make up the rest of the cost
of the weir. Not to mention the twelve shillings a day
for those working the road, and the tools we will need
to give them to do the work. And what with the other

schemes you have begun, it will not be long before you spend the budget you gave me."

"You may leave that to me," Kilgarvan said, repressing a sigh. He had already reached the same conclusion. The marriage settlements had paid off his debts, and included the sum of one thousand pounds for improvements to the estate. That would not be enough for the changes he wished to make, and yet to spend more he would need the concurrence of his wife.

It would feel very much like begging, and he felt a surge of self-loathing, and anger toward his father, who had placed him in this impossible position. If his father had not squandered his inheritance, he would never have been in such a position of dependence.

He did not know how Felicity would react when he asked her for more funds. Would the trust and friendship they had developed during their journey survive? Or would the money come between them again, as it had at the start of their marriage? He closed his eyes, feeling a moment of despair as he realized that he might never be free of the millstone of debt and responsibility that held him chained.

Felicity was furious with Kilgarvan for leaving her alone in her new home with strangers while he rushed away. Surely there was no estate business so urgent that he could not have stayed long enough to see her settled, and to show her around his home.

Instead she stood in the bare, empty entrance hall, in the company of two women, whom Kilgarvan had introduced as Mrs. O'Connor and her daughter Bridget, along with the comment that they were the

mother and sister of Dennis O'Connor, whom she
had just met. Mrs. O'Connor was a short, plump
woman, with graying hair and a round, cheerful face.
Her daughter Bridget was a thinner and younger ver-
sion of her mother. She had the same cheerful face
and ready smile. Both wore dresses of a dark blue
wool, and spotless white linen aprons. Mrs. O'Connor had a cap as well, and a set of keys tied around
her belt. Their attire was far superior to that of the
ordinary villagers Felicity had just seen.

"Isn't that just like himself, to be rushing off without scarce time to catch his breath," Mrs. O'Connor
said. "And you the stranger here, and wondering
what it is that you have let yourself in for."

Her words echoed Felicity's sentiments exactly. "Indeed," she said. "And not even a proper introduction. Am I to assume that you are the housekeeper?"

"Ah, no, though I may as well be for now. We haven't
had a housekeeper here for near a dozen years, not
since the countess's last visit. Nora Murphy does the
cooking, and cleans for himself when she gets the notion, and her sister does the washing, but beyond that,
there's nothing been done." She lowered her voice a
bit and leaned forward as if to impart confidential
information. "It was just the two gentlemen, and then
the old earl died, God rest his soul, and naught but
young Gerald left. And he was never one to spend
money on luxuries."

"But you were the housekeeper before?" Felicity
asked.

Mrs. O'Connor laughed. "And sure I thought you
knew this all along. My husband was the agent for
the old lord, before his death, and my son Dennis is
his agent now. When Dennis learned Kilgarvan was
bringing home a bride, he asked me to see to things

until you could find a proper staff. The village women are willing enough, but most have no training, and none of them speak English."

Mrs. O'Connor observed her shrewdly, and Felicity knew that she was being summed up. It was apparent that none of them, not Kilgarvan, not his family and certainly not his dependents, had expected her to wish to live in the wilds of Ireland with her husband. After seeing Glenmore and the countryside of Kilgarvan, she could well understand their doubts. She could not picture the dowager countess in such a setting.

"Well, I am grateful for your help," Felicity said. "And now, if you would be so kind as to show me around. After such long neglect, I am certain there is much to be done, and we should start at once."

"What would you like to see, my lady?"

"Everything," Felicity said firmly.

Mrs. O'Connor turned to her daughter. "Bridget, tell Nora Murphy that I am with the countess, and that she is to see to a proper dinner for the earl and his wife. And then find the O'Hanlon sisters. They should have been finished scrubbing those floors an hour ago. See that they are not slacking off, and lend them a hand if they need it."

"Yes, mum," Bridget said.

"If you would come this way, my lady?" Mrs. O'Connor said, indicating the grand stairs. "The upper floors are the worst, so we can begin there."

Felicity learned that Arlyn Court had been built only forty years before by Kilgarvan's grandfather. Made out of local blue-gray limestone, it had been designed as a central block, following the fashion of the time. Flanking the entranceway were two small receiving rooms. An elaborately carved mahogany

staircase led up to the second floor. The east end was
given over to the bedrooms for the family. Felicity
found that two bedrooms had been made up, one
for her and one for Kilgarvan. The two rooms connected through a shared sitting room, which held a
beautiful view of the lake.

It was obvious that the rooms had been well
cleaned and aired, yet even as she complimented
Mrs. O'Connor on their appearance she found herself wondering if Kilgarvan would share her bed tonight, or if she would sleep alone.

On the west end were bedrooms for guests, and at
the far end was the nursery. These rooms were in
even poorer shape than the master bedrooms. The
drapes were threadbare, the wallpaper faded and
peeling. Most rooms lacked rugs of any sort, and she
would wager the floors had not been waxed in years.

In one room the wall was stained, showing where
water had leaked in at some point. The floor in that
corner was slightly warped, and Mrs. O'Connor explained that no one had noticed the leak for days,
perhaps weeks, so seldom did anyone venture to this
part of the mansion.

Save for the earl's chamber, the rooms felt chill and
empty. There were no pictures, no flowers, no knick-
knacks or curios. Felicity felt an absurd urge to whisper.

Above the second floor were small attics, with quarters for servants, though there were none living there
at the present, Nora Murphy and her helpers prefer-
ring to live in the village.

Descending the staircase, they examined the first
floor. On the east side, beyond the small reception
room, was a larger salon, and beyond that was the
dining room. It was clear that the maids had been

busy here, for the mahogany table shone glossy and bright.

The west side of the house held a library whose shelves were forlornly empty. Connected to the library was a music room, although no instrument stood within. Beyond that was a small room that had served as a breakfast room when the countess was in residence. And at the south end of the house was an enormous drawing room with large glass windows that looked out onto a small terrace, from which twin staircases led down into a terraced garden. The gardens, like everything else, had been much neglected. Mrs. O'Connor lamented the fine roses that had grown here when she was a girl.

Returning inside, they descended to the lowest floor, which held the kitchens, pantry and servants' hall. It could be more properly called the cellar, and although the north end of the building held no windows and was virtually underground, the kitchen was in the south end, and had the advantages of windows to provide sunlight and fresh air.

Felicity accepted Mrs. O'Connor's offer of a cup of tea, and joined her in what had been the housekeeper's room, just off the kitchen.

"So what do you think?" Mrs. O'Connor asked after they had each sipped their tea.

"It is not as bad as I expected. You and your helpers must have worked very hard to get all this ready in such a short time."

Mrs. O'Connor beamed. "And I thank you for your praise. But shame on us if we didn't have things set to rights. We've been working on this for over a month, since Dennis came back from London with the news that the earl was to be married."

So Dennis O'Connor had been with her husband

in London. The two were of an age, and from what Mrs. O'Connor had said, it was likely that they were friends rather than simply employer and employee. But if so, why had he not come to their wedding? For surely Kilgarvan would have introduced them, had he been there. It was a puzzle, but one she could solve later.

Felicity put the thought from her mind. She had more important matters to think about. Arlyn Court needed a firm hand if it were to be made a fitting residence again. Fortunately this was a task with which she had experience. Many times she had set up housekeeping in a strange land with her father. Arlyn Court was hardly the worst she had seen. And this time she had the satisfaction of knowing that she would be here to enjoy the fruits of her labors.

She could hardly wait to get started. But a glance at her watch showed that the afternoon was nearly gone, and soon it would be time for dinner.

"We will start by making lists tomorrow," Felicity said. "And I'll need recommendations from you. We'll need to hire more servants to finish the cleaning, and to begin painting and making repairs. And we should make a list of things we need from Cork."

Remembering the poverty of the villagers, she resolved to hire as many servants as she could find tasks for.

"There are plenty of folks who are willing to work," Mrs. O'Connor said. "But my Dennis said the earl had authorized only a small staff. Mayhap you'll want to talk with him before you begin."

Felicity shook her head firmly. "No, there is no need to trouble Kilgarvan with this. I am sure he has enough to occupy himself with the estate. Restoring the house is my task, and I have funds enough of my own that we need not trouble him."

"It has been a long time since Arlyn Court had a countess," Mrs. O'Connor said.

"But surely his lordship's mother—"

"Her ladyship is a Dublin woman," Mrs. O'Connor said with a sniff of disdain. "Meaning no disrespect, but she was never happy here. She stayed here in the beginning, when Master Gerald was a baby and the marriage was new. Then each year she spent more and more time in Dublin, until one year she did not return at all. No, what the house has always needed is a proper countess, one who knows the way of setting things right."

"That is something I can do," Felicity replied.

Fourteen

It was nearly full dark when Kilgarvan returned to Arlyn Court, and Felicity was fuming. How dared he treat her so? He had told her that he would return soon, after he had a word with his agent. Assured by Mrs. O'Connor that the earl kept country hours, at sunset she had dressed for dinner. But there had been no sign of her husband.

Felicity sat in the front parlor, which held a good view of the path from the village. She sat and waited. Mrs. O'Connor kept her company for a bit, until Felicity could no longer bear the speculation she saw in the woman's eyes. So she dismissed the housekeeper, saying there was no sense in both of them missing their dinners. She watched from the window as Mrs. O'Connor walked toward Glenmore, following the path her daughter had taken earlier.

The golden sunset gave way to pale gray twilight, and still there was no sign of her husband, no message telling her that he was delayed. She wondered bleakly if he intended to come home at all, or if he planned to stay away for the night.

She had so looked forward to this first dinner together, the start of their life together in what was to be their home. But as the clock tolled the hours, her anticipation turned to anger. Unable to sit, she paced back and forth in the parlor, rehearsing the dressing-down she would give Kilgarvan when she saw him.

As the clock struck nine, she decided she could take it no more. She would go to Glenmore and find what was keeping her husband. And if it was another woman, she would cheerfully wring both their necks. But first she had to change her attire. Her flimsy slippers and evening gown would serve her ill on her expedition.

She was halfway up the stairs when she heard the door open behind her. She continued her march.

"Felicity," he called.

She turned and saw him standing in the entrance. The few candles lit threw dark shadows, and if not for his voice, she would not have known who it was who stood there.

"Where have you been?" she demanded.

"Out," he said. There was a long pause as he closed the door behind him and stepped into the pool of light in the main hallway. "I am sorry I am late," he added.

Angry words trembled at the tip of her tongue, but she bit them back as she caught a glimpse of his face. Kilgarvan's face was set in grim lines, revealing his unhappiness, and his carriage drooped with exhaustion. She felt a sudden rush of sympathy.

"There is time to wash up, if you like," she said. "And if there is anything left of dinner, I will ask Nora Murphy to bring it to the dining room."

Her jest produced only the faintest of smiles. "That would be kind," he said.

Felicity ventured into the kitchen, where Nora Murphy waved a spoon as she berated her at length. Though Felicity did not speak Gaelic, she had experience enough of cooks to know that Nora was complaining of the impossibility of preparing decent food under these conditions. Felicity ignored the tirade, and invoked her husband's name in a firm voice. Eventually the cook nodded and began to place items on a tray, muttering under her breath all the while.

The dining room, which had looked so fine in the sunlight, appeared forbidding and lonely in the evening. The few tallow candles sputtered and threw gloomy shadows. Kilgarvan sat at the head of the table, and Felicity to his right. The table seemed absurdly long for just the two of them, and Felicity fought the odd urge to whisper in the darkness.

Candles, she reminded herself. Hundreds of wax candles would be ordered from Cork, and would bring a little cheer to this dismal place.

The food was plain, but good, and Kilgarvan devoured his with speed. Felicity ate her own meal, albeit more slowly. Then again, she had had the advantage of taking tea this afternoon, while from the looks of it Kilgarvan had eaten nothing since that morning.

She let him eat in silence, knowing from experience that gentlemen were ill-disposed to reason when they were hungry. At last Kilgarvan pushed his plate away, and she rose, stacking the dishes on a tray. She placed the tray on the sideboard for the cook to fetch later.

She thought about suggesting they retire to another room, but she had no doubt that the other public rooms would be equally gloomy. So instead she poured a fresh glass of wine for each of them, and resumed her seat.

Kilgarvan grasped the stem of the glass and turned

it slowly between two fingers, as if admiring the delicate crystal. Then he raised his eyes to her.

"I should not have left you alone here," he said. "You must think me discourteous indeed."

"I would have preferred to have you show me around Arlyn Court," she admitted. "But Mrs. O'Connor was an excellent guide."

"And what do you think?"

His eyes were dark and hooded, and she found it difficult to know what he was thinking.

"It is a fine house," she said. "I am sure it was beautiful once, and it will be so again, once we have a chance to air out the rooms and give them the benefit of new paint and new furnishings. I thought to hire some workers from the village, and Mrs. O'Connor has promised to come over tomorrow to help me draw up a list of what we need to order from Cork."

Kilgarvan looked doubtful. "The servants are a good idea, I suppose. If nothing else, the families will be grateful for the employment. And you can send to Cork or Killarney for any provisions you need— Dennis O'Connor can make the arrangements. But I had not thought to spend money on decorating or furniture or other frills," he said. "Not until the estates begin to produce again."

"They are not frills. The roof is leaking in the south corner—did you know that? And Mrs. O'Connor said the linens are in a dreadful state."

Kilgarvan looked uncertain, so she pressed her point home. "You need not worry about the expense," she said. "Do you not remember that my uncle gave us five hundred pounds as a wedding present to use for setting up our establishment? No doubt he thought we intended to live in Dublin or London, but there is no reason why we can't use the money here."

"Very well," he said. "But we may find a better use for that five hundred pounds before long."

"Is that what has you looking so grim this evening?"

He raised one hand and rubbed his temples as if his head pained him. "You saw it for yourself. The estate is tottering on the brink of ruin."

"Is all of Kilgarvan in such poor shape?"

He gave a grim laugh. "Worse. Those in Glenmore are better off than many," he said.

She did not want to imagine what could be worse than the conditions she had seen in the village that afternoon.

"How did this happen? Was it a sudden calamity?"

He took a sip of his wine. "The calamity was the late Earl of Kilgarvan," he said bitterly. "In my grandfather's time this was a prosperous estate, rich enough so that he could tear down the old manor and build Arlyn Court for his new bride. And then my father inherited, and he was not satisfied with simply having a good estate and a comfortable living. He wanted a showplace, to compete with the great estates of the north."

Kilgarvan shook his head from side to side, in condemnation of his father's folly. "At first he was convinced that these hills must be full of lead and tin, as they are to the west. He spent a fortune sinking mine shafts, with nothing to show for it. And then there was the canal company he invested in, which went bankrupt. Other schemes followed, each as useless as the last. When he could no longer afford to pay for them from his income, he began mortgaging the estate. Till the end, he was convinced that one of his schemes would prosper, and that Kilgarvan would reclaim its former glory."

"And he left you with the burden of his debts," Felicity said, reaching over and squeezing his hand in sympathy.

"There is so much to do that I don't even know where to start," he confessed. "I thought once my debts were cleared that I could manage, but now I do not know."

She could see the pain in his face, and she felt renewed admiration for him. She did not know any other man who cared as deeply for his people and felt his responsibilities so keenly. But Kilgarvan was only one man, and even he needed to lay down his burden sometime.

"Come," she said, rising but not relinquishing his hand. "You need your rest. Tomorrow is soon enough to begin."

He gave her a weary smile and rose. Lifting her hand to his lips, he brushed it with a kiss. "I bow to your wisdom," he said.

Holding her hand in his, with his other hand he retrieved a candle from the sideboard. Then he led the way upstairs. At the door of her bedroom she paused, uncertain how to ask the question that was uppermost in her mind.

He tugged her hand. "Will you lie with me tonight?" he asked.

"Yes," she said, suddenly breathless with anticipation and a sense of relief. When Kilgarvan had not returned home today, she had begun to fear that he had regretted what had happened between them the night before. But now as his thumb gently stroked the pulse in her wrist, she realized how foolish she had been. Their marriage might have had a poor start, but that was behind them now.

He made love to her with a feverish intensity that belied his earlier tiredness. His touch awoke a fierce hunger in her, akin to and yet somehow different from the gentle passion they had shared the previous night. Their climax was shattering in its intensity, and Kilgarvan soon fell into an exhausted slumber. But she remained awake, feeling his heart beat against her chest, and holding him in her arms as if she could keep trouble at bay.

The next morning Kilgarvan left after breakfast, pleading the press of estate business. He promised to return at a civilized hour for dinner, and with this, Felicity had to be content.

Mrs. O'Connor arrived soon afterward, along with half a dozen young men and women from the village. Felicity hired the workers on the spot; then, with Mrs. O'Connor translating her instructions, she set them to work.

Felicity and Mrs. O'Connor spent the day inventorying Arlyn Court. They went room by room, examining everything. Furniture, carpets, drapes, bed linens, all were carefully inspected. And they made endless lists. There was a list of rooms to be cleaned, and in which order. Lists of furniture that needed repair, drapes to be mended or replaced, bed linens and flannels to be ordered.

"These are not fit for cleaning rags," Felicity said, shaking her head as she closed the door to the linen closet. Though she had paid little attention last night, in daylight she had realized that the sheets on Kilgarvan's bed had frayed edges. And having inspected the linen closet she realized that those indeed had been the finest sheets in the house. Most of the rest were so worn and mended that they seemed in danger of falling apart. "We'll have to replace them all. Best order two dozen sets, and then we'll see as we go on."

"It will be cheaper to buy the fabric, and have the girls make them up for you," Mrs. O'Connor offered.

"No, we'll have more than enough to keep them busy. They could work from dawn till dusk for the next two months, and still not accomplish everything on our lists."

The task before them was daunting, yet instead of feeling discouraged, Felicity was energized by what she had discovered. Here, at last, was a project that she could turn her hand to, one that would require all her skills and talents. Arlyn Court needed her, and it was a feeling that she welcomed.

She wondered if Kilgarvan's attachment to his land stemmed from the same realization of how much he was needed here. And she realized how frustrated he must have felt when he realized that all his dedication and love for his people were not enough to save them.

"Ah, you have the right of it there," Mrs. O'Connor said, breaking into her train of thought. "But it will do the girls good to keep themselves from idleness, and for them to see how a proper house is run."

Leaving behind the first floor, they sought out the kitchens. There they found Nora Murphy busy with preparations for dinner.

"I would like to inspect the larder, to see what is needed," Felicity said, then waited while Mrs. O'Connor translated her words.

With a speed surprising in one her age, the cook

moved from the cutting table to stand in front of the larder, barring the way.

"Step aside," Felicity ordered.

The cook unleashed a torrent of Gaelic, her dark eyes flashing. Mrs. O'Connor replied in the same tongue. A heated exchange followed. Felicity was frustrated by her inability to understand what was being discussed at such volume, though from the gestures it was clear that the cook felt insulted by their inspection.

She would have to get Kilgarvan to teach her Gaelic, she decided. She could not rely upon Mrs. O'Connor forever, and it was impossible to run a house where the servants could not understand her, and she could not understand them.

"Tell her that if she wishes to remain as cook, she will do as I ask. At once."

For a moment Felicity thought that the cook would refuse, and then with a toss of her head, the woman stepped aside.

The larder was windowless and dark, the light from the kitchen penetrating no more than a few inches inside the door.

"A lamp, if you would be so kind," Felicity said.

Mrs. O'Connor left, and in a few moments returned with a burning lamp. Holding it in front of her, Felicity entered.

The larder was a long, narrow room. Built into the wall on one side was a work counter, with drawers and cabinets underneath. On the other side were shelves, with containers of flour, corn meal, sugar, spices and the like. Toward the back, a large bushel basket held potatoes, while a smaller basket next to it held carrots.

It was cleaner than she had expected, if a trifle

empty. They wouldn't starve, but any food served would be of the plain variety, at least until they received their first order of provisions from Cork. Felicity suspected that she would soon grow mightily tired of potatoes.

There was naught amiss, save that supplies were low. From the cook's attitude she had half expected to find jugs of Irish whiskey or other signs of misuse of Kilgarvan's money.

Emerging from the pantry, she blew out the lamp and placed it on the work counter. The cook's eyes followed her suspiciously, her cheeks flushed with anger.

"Please tell the cook to make a list of what she needs, and I will include it in the order I send to Cork."

"Ah, the auld thing does not write, but I will get her to tell me what we need, and make the list for her," Mrs. O'Connor offered.

"Very well," Felicity said.

As she left the kitchen, she felt weary, but she also felt a certain sense of satisfaction. It would take months if not years to put Arlyn Court to rights. But she had made a good start today, and she knew herself the equal to the task. She owed it to herself, and to her husband, to make this a place they could feel proud of, and where they could raise a family.

Fifteen

It hardly seemed possible that it had been a week since Kilgarvan's return to Glenmore. Each day had been busier than the last.

He had toured the cabins owned by the estate, and decided which should be repaired and which should be torn down. He had settled the quarrel over the ownership of the black cow, along with a score of other petty disputes that had arisen during the six months of his absence.

He had discussed the rents with Jerry O'Connell, and who should be allowed to lease land that had fallen idle. He had heard Father Harrington's plea for a new roof for the chapel, and instructed the workers who were erecting the new schoolhouse.

The arrival of Mr. Hamilton had proven another distraction. An acquaintance from his school days in Dublin, Mr. Hamilton congratulated Kilgarvan on his good fortune, and listened intently as Kilgarvan explained his plans for the estate. Like most Irish, teaching was only one of Hamilton's trades, and since school would not begin till the fall, Kilgarvan had set Mr. Hamilton to work surveying the land for the new cottages.

A week after his return to Glenmore, Kilgarvan

joined his wife for breakfast. But instead of hurrying off on estate business, as had been his custom, he asked her to accompany him on a stroll. Felicity readily agreed, seeming pleased at the prospect of spending time in his company. Such opportunities had been all too rare since his homecoming, as matters both great and small had demanded his attention.

It was a fine day, and he waited for her outside while Felicity consulted with Mrs. O'Connor and left instructions. Mentally he rehearsed what he would say to her, but before he could make sense of his arguments, Felicity appeared.

She was wearing a straw bonnet trimmed with a dark blue ribbon that matched her muslin walking dress. She had exchanged her house slippers for stylish half boots, the very same boots that she had worn for their journey here. As she descended the stairs to the lawn, he could see the faintest trace of freckles on the bridge of her nose.

"It is a beautiful day for a stroll," she said. "And it was so lovely of you to think of this. It seems I've been cooped up in the house for days."

She smiled happily, and he wished with all his heart that he had indeed made this offer simply because it would please her.

"Did you have a destination in mind, or are we simply to enjoy the fine day?"

"There is something I want to show you," he said, offering her his arm. "Down by the lake."

Felicity began telling him of Arlyn Court, and the changes that she was making. He listened with only a part of his mind, murmuring agreement when it seemed appropriate.

Their path took them through the village, then west, across the stone bridge that arched over the stream that drained from the lake. Then they proceeded along the west bank of the lake. The woods came quite near the lakeshore on this side, but there was a path, of sorts, and as they approached the ruined castle the woods gave way to open meadowlands.

"Don't you agree?" Felicity asked.

"Er, yes, of course."

Felicity laughed, a warm, infectious sound. "You haven't been paying the least attention to what I was saying," she accused. "I just suggested that we should turn the grand salon into a cattle barn, and you agreed."

He smiled as an image sprang to mind of the grand salon filled with a dozen black cattle executing the steps of the quadrille, with himself and Felicity standing on the sidelines, smiling their approval.

"I apologize. My mind was wandering," he said. "And while we do need a new barn, I do not think we are that desperate. Yet."

The moment of mirth passed as quickly as it had come, for the new barn was just one of the things he needed to discuss with Felicity.

"Is it much farther?" she asked.

"Are you weary?"

"No, but it is clear you will not be fit for conversation until we have seen whatever it is you want me to see."

"Just a bit farther," he promised.

As they entered the meadow, they had their first clear glimpse of the old castle. Once it was a mighty fortress; now only the central tower and the crumbling remains of the inner wall remained. The gray stone was scarred from cannon shot, and though he could not see it from here, the inside of the keep was still blackened from the fire that had raged when the keep was set to the torch.

The years had taken their toll, and where once warriors had stood guard, now cattle wandered among the grass that had overtaken the crumbled stones, or lay dozing in the shade of the walls.

"This is Arlyn Castle? From your description I expected a ruin, but this is marvelous. One almost expects to see brave knights on the field, and fair damsels waving to them from the parapet," she said fancifully.

She tugged his arm, but he did not budge, and so she relinquished his hand and went ahead eagerly. He followed behind at a more sedate pace.

"Careful," he called. "The footing can be treacherous. The grass is full of stones, scattered from when the outer wall was breached."

He caught up with her as she paused beside the ruined gate, gazing up at the central tower. "Strange, the tower does not appear at all harmed," she mused.

"Appearances can be deceiving. The tower was set to the torch. The walls still stand, but there was nothing left inside."

"And this was your family's?"

He nodded. "Arlyn Castle, the seat of the earls of Kilgarvan. That is, until my ancestor joined the rebellion. Cromwell's army made short work of them, and my ancestor forfeited his title and lands."

"But—" she began, puzzlement in her voice.

"His eldest son was allowed to swear fealty to the Crown, and had the title and some of the lands restored. But the castle was gone forever, as was the eastern half of the valley. My ancestor swore that someday we would reclaim the land they had lost. But it remains an empty promise."

"And is that what you wish as well? To reclaim this all?"

"No."

His father had inherited the dream of past glories. It had been the seed that fueled his desire for ever grander schemes to bring wealth and the old glory back to the Kilgarvan name. But it had been a fool's dream, and had brought ruin instead. Now Kilgarvan would be content merely to hold on to what he had, and to see it prosper.

He turned his back on the castle and looked back down at the lake. From here the end of the lake could be plainly seen, as well as the village of Glenmore. He took a deep breath, and then began.

"I did not come here to talk about castles," he said. "I wanted to show you this meadow. There are over two hundred acres here of good, level land. It has been idle too long. What I propose is building cabins here. A dozen this year, and then another dozen the next. Each tenant would receive twenty acres of land for cultivation. We would offer long leases, with a modest rent at first, and then increase the rent as the land began to yield crops."

Felicity gazed around the meadow, her brow wrinkling as if she was trying to picture what he had described. "You are proposing a village similar to what Lord Shelbourne has done in Nedeen, am I not right?"

"Yes, but how did you know of Nedeen?"

"Arthur Young described the project in his essays," she said absently. "I take it you have given this some thought?"

"Mr. Hamilton has already completed the preliminary surveys," he admitted.

"I see."

He could not tell what she was thinking.

She slowly walked a few paces away, increasing the distance between them. Then she turned.

"Did you invite me here to ask my opinion? Or simply because you need my approval for the expenditure?"

His silence was answer enough.

"Are there any other projects you have begun that I should know of?" Her tone was deceptively mild, but he knew she was angry.

His eyes fell before the heat of her gaze. "The cabins in Glenmore are in terrible condition. Some of them will be razed, as the tenants move into the new cottages we build here. But others need repairs now, before the winter approaches."

"I assume you know how much all this is to cost?"

"Five thousand pounds, or thereabouts," he said. The words were as ashes in his mouth. He felt as if he were begging.

There was a long pause.

"I will take a look at the plans," she said. "And if they seem reasonable, then I will instruct Mr. Clutterbuck to release the funds."

She gave him a sideways glance. "Five thousand pounds seems a high price for what you have described. Is there anything else you have neglected to mention? The fishing weir, perhaps? Or the money to pay the crews repairing the roads?"

He gritted his teeth. "Those, too, of course. And while you are in the mood to open your purse, should I tell you that Father Harrington has asked for a new roof for the chapel, and that the schoolhouse will be needing desks and chairs, as well as books for the pupils? Not to mention the new cattle byre, which we

will need before the winter, to protect the bloodstock
that Dennis O'Connor is off fetching.''

"Enough," she said. "You can present me with a
full accounting of what you propose to spend, and I
will review it. You do not even need to speak to me,
if you find it a bother. Just leave the list with one of
the servants, and I will get to it in my own good time.''

The tone of her voice was matched by the anger
on her face. He knew she was angry that he had not
seen fit to consult her first. But what right had she
to be angry? He was the one who was forced to beg
for every farthing to spend, as if he were a child or
a lackwit.

She was the one who had made this impossible
agreement, and who showed no signs of relinquishing control of her purse strings.

His own anger rose. It was demeaning that he
should have to beg like this, seeking his wife's approval over every pound spent, as if he were a spend-
thrift or lackwit. Each word was like poison gall, and
yet Felicity made the task no easier with her insistence
that he explain every last farthing to her. What did
she know of Glenmore, or Kilgarvan, or even of Ireland, for that matter? By her own account she had
lived the life of a vagabond, never pausing in one
place long enough to watch the seasons change. And
yet she presumed to lecture him on how best to care
for his tenants, a woman who had not set foot on her
own family's land for eighteen years.

The walk back to Arlyn Court was quiet indeed.

That night, for the first time in a week, Felicity slept
alone. Not that she would have welcomed Kilgarvan's
presence. Indeed, she might have spurned him, so

great had been her temper. But as the hours dragged on and there was no tap at her door, Felicity felt a chill seep into her heart.

He did not love her. He had never loved her. She was just a convenience, a wife who came with an ample dowry. How surprised he must have been to have found pleasure in their marriage bed. But that in itself did not prove that he valued her as a person— merely that he found her comely, and in the fashion of men everywhere, was prepared to take advantage of what she had so naively offered.

A part of her clung to the belief that there had been something special in his regard for her. Some tenderness, and perhaps even passion. But as the clock ticked softly, and the candle sputtered and died, such thoughts could not comfort her. Whatever closeness they shared in bed could not bridge the gap that had grown between them during their waking hours.

All her efforts at friendship and tolerance—those were as naught. Kilgarvan was still angry over the marriage settlement, and unwilling to see her as anything more than a source of funds.

How easy it would have been for him to ask her advice about the new village. Apparently he had had no problem sharing his plans with the schoolteacher, who had surveyed the land. Discreet questioning of Mrs. O'Connor revealed that she knew of—and heartily approved—the scheme. According to the housekeeper, lists of prospective tenants were already being drawn up.

It seemed that everyone in Glenmore, and in the surrounding lands of Kilgarvan, knew what her husband was planning.

Everyone except his wife.

And this was the source of her anger and dismay. It was not the money. She gladly would have given him ten thousand pounds, or fifty, if it was needed. If only he had asked, instead of demanded, in his stiff-necked way.

Briefly she considered denying him the funds. But satisfying as it would be to cast Kilgarvan's rudeness back in his face, she could not do so. New cottages were desperately needed, no matter how arrogant and insufferable their lord was.

All she wanted was to be included in Kilgarvan, to feel that she was part of the splendid new beginning that was being made. But as estate matters consumed more and more of her husband's time, he shut her out more. He had time for everyone except her.

Which was why she had been so happy this morning when he asked for her company. And then he had ruined the occasion with his ill-chosen words.

It was as if he were deliberately trying to drive a stake between them, to keep her at arm's length. But that made no sense either.

During the journey from Cork, she had thought that they had reached an understanding, and that this would set the pattern of their days. But what if she had been wrong? What if the journey had been simply an interlude? One where Kilgarvan had felt free to cast off his cares, and to accept the friendship that she offered. And now, the interlude passed, Kilgarvan had resumed his old habits—habits that did not include sharing any part of his life with his new wife.

She smiled grimly as she realized the irony of her thoughts. In truth, when she had proposed marriage, she had envisioned a life much as the one she led now: a conventional marriage based on mutual respect, and adherence to duty. A life where husband and wife each had their spheres of influence, which rarely overlapped.

And yet, having seen the possibility that there could be so much more, she was now unwilling to settle for what Kilgarvan seemed prepared to offer.

Sixteen

The next morning, Kilgarvan was nowhere to be found. Questioning the maid who served breakfast proved a futile task, since the girl spoke no English. All Felicity could gather was that Kilgarvan was not in the house, but when he had left and where he had gone was a riddle.

This was absolutely ridiculous, she fumed. She could not run a house where she could not speak to the servants. But as it was, she was forced to wait for Mrs. O'Connor to arrive so she could relay her requests to the servants.

After consulting with Mrs. O'Connor on the day's tasks, and leaving instructions that she was to be notified as soon as Kilgarvan returned, Felicity retired to her sitting room. There she drafted orders for provisions and furnishings from Cork, and authorized the payment of tradesmen's bills. After some consideration, she also drafted a letter to her solicitor, Mr. Clutterbuck, authorizing him to release the five thousand pounds Kilgarvan had requested. She was still angry over Kilgarvan's high-handedness, but she could not deny that the money was indeed desperately needed.

The remainder of the morning was spent in the

kitchen discussing menus with Nora Murphy. The cook bristled at Felicity's suggestion, as relayed through Mrs. O'Connor, that perhaps it was time to expand the menus. The suggestion that every meal need not include potatoes was met with stark incredulity and a muttered stream of invective that Mrs. O'Connor refused to translate.

But Felicity stood firm, and reminded Mrs. Murphy that if she felt unequal to the challenge, then Felicity would simply send to Dublin to advertise for a cook with experience in serving a noble house. This earned her a glare, followed by a grudging promise that the cook would do her best to comply with her ladyship's wishes.

Felicity left the kitchen to the sound of clanging pots and muttered complaints.

"Pay no mind to auld Nora," Mrs. O'Connor said. "She is set in her ways, but she will come around in time."

"I hope so," Felicity said, though privately she had her doubts. Mrs. Murphy had glared at her so strongly that she suspected tonight's meal might be burned, or worse yet, consist solely of potatoes. "After her long service it would be a shame if we had to give her notice. But I have my standards, and if Nora Murphy cannot live up to them, then we will simply have to find her another position."

After the confrontation with the cook, Mrs. O'Connor excused herself to return to her duties. With no tasks that urgently required her attention, Felicity decided to take a short stroll outside.

From the south side of the house, the great double staircase descended from the portico to the first of six terraces that followed the gentle slope of the hill. Each level had a large rectangular raised flower bed

in the center, flanked on either side by smaller beds.
Gravel pathways separated the beds, and stone steps
led from one level to another.

A few hardy roses still grew in the center bed, but
years of neglect had taken their toll. Most of the beds
were overgrown with weeds and bracken. Ornamental bushes had grown so large they could no longer
be seen over. In places the gravel paths had washed
away or been overgrown by grass.

She paused on the lowermost level, looking back
up toward the house, closing her eyes for a moment
as she tried to imagine how it would look once the
beds had been redone and the flowers were in bloom.

Then she opened her eyes. It had been beautiful
once, and she knew she could make it so again. But
it would be an enormous task, and there was already
so much else that needed to be done. There were
not enough hours in the day to oversee all the improvements being made at Arlyn Court. And what
laborers were not currently employed in renovating
the house would be needed for the building projects
that Kilgarvan had planned.

She sighed. She had always wanted a place with her
own gardens, where she could stay long enough to
plant flowers and see them bloom. She had never
had that kind of security, that sense of belonging that
came with knowing that she would have a chance to
see the fruits of her labors.

But there were so many more urgent matters that
required immediate attention. She could hardly ask
men to work on ornamental gardens when their own
cottages were in danger of falling down on their
heads. She could wait. Perhaps next spring there
would be time for her to fulfill this dream.

"This used to be so beautiful in the summer," a voice said, echoing her thoughts.

She whirled and saw that Kilgarvan had come up behind her, the sound of his approach masked by the soft grass. He moved forward to stand beside her, his arms clasped loosely behind his back as he surveyed the garden.

"With time and effort we can make it bloom again," she promised. "If not this year, then the next."

He nodded, but he still looked grave—and tired, with shadows under his eyes that revealed that his night had been no more restful than hers.

"There is a letter for Mr. Clutterbuck in your study," Felicity said. "He is instructed to make the funds you requested available to Mr. Perry."

"Thank you," he said stiffly, his face assuming the shuttered look that it always wore whenever they discussed money.

An awkward silence stretched between them. Kilgarvan turned as if he would leave, but she placed her hand on his arm before he could make his escape.

"I would like to see the plans for the new village, and to discuss them with you before you begin building," she said.

"You may not trust my judgment, but you can trust Mr. Hamilton," Kilgarvan said. "The project is simple enough, and he has wide experience in surveying."

"I was not criticizing you," she said, wondering why Kilgarvan was so prickly. Even the most innocent of comments was interpreted by him as an attack on him or a slur on his judgment. "But there is no harm in another set of eyes. Seeing the plans will make me feel a part of what you are doing. And I may be able to suggest something that you have not thought of."

"If you insist."

"I do. And there is another thing," she said. "I cannot be running to Mrs. O'Connor every time I need to speak to one of the servants. I need someone to teach me Gaelic. I know you are busy, but I promise I am a fast learner."

"No," Kilgarvan said.

"Why ever not?"

"It would be better for them if they learned to speak English," Kilgarvan said. "That is why I asked Mr. Hamilton to come, to start the school."

"But Gaelic is their native tongue. You speak it. Why should not I?" Was this yet another attempt of his to exclude her from his life and his people? How often did she have to prove herself to him?

"They can learn Gaelic at home," Kilgarvan said. "But English is the language of commerce. A man who knows only Gaelic is destined for poverty. Only the lowest of jobs are open to him. He cannot bargain fairly with the merchants in Cork for his goods, nor can he understand the bargains that are offered him. Far better for them all to learn English so they can prosper."

She stared at him, unable to believe he could be so blind. "What you say may be true, but that does not make it right. The people of Kilgarvan are my people too, now, and the least their countess can do is to master a few words of their language. If you will not teach me, then I will simply ask Mr. Hamilton instead."

"You can do as you like. But then again, you always do as you please, don't you?" Kilgarvan retorted.

Then, before she could summon up strength for an insult, he was gone.

Kilgarvan bit down hard on his anger. He knew he had been rude to Felicity, but it was her fault for provoking him. Lately her every comment seemed to have a double meaning, a hidden barb.

After yesterday's quarrel, he had expected that she would refuse to release the funds, or would release only part of the sum he had requested. And so this morning he had spent in the village with Dennis O'Connor, trying to decide what they could afford to do with what remained of the thousand pounds he had received as the wedding settlement.

Then she had surprised him by giving him all that he had asked for. But his gratitude did not last long, for with one hand she gave, while with the other she took. The price of her money was her interference, her constant questioning of his judgment, her insistence that she knew better than he did what was right for his land and his people.

Her words grated against his nerves, in part because he had begun to doubt himself. Restoring Kilgarvan to prosperity was an enormous undertaking. It was not enough simply to fix up a handful of cottages, or to provide a lucky few with employment as servants or laborers. No, what was needed here was a sustainable economy. Enterprises that did not depend upon agriculture, or upon the size of the earl's purse to provide employment for all. To do this would require years, perhaps even a decade or more.

And over his hopes and plans hung the memory of his father's failures. The late earl had not been a bad man, or even a greedy one. Just unwise when it came to managing his affairs. But was his son any better? Clearly his wife did not think so.

He could still remember the horror in her eyes when she had seen the poverty of Glenmore. Nothing would erase that memory from his mind, nor of the sick shame he felt when he had beheld her shock.

And so he threw himself into overseeing every detail of his projects, not daring to trust anyone else with this responsibility. He sought advice from Dennis O'Connor and Mr. Hamilton, but in the end the responsibility was his, for good or for ill.

He felt his stomach clench as he promised himself that he would not fail. He could not. He would spend every last ounce of his energy making right what was wrong.

The next weeks passed in an uneasy truce. Kilgarvan spent more and more of his time away from the house. Felicity knew he was avoiding her, but when she raised this objection, he claimed that it was simply the press of his duties that kept him away from her. And in truth he was busy, returning to Arlyn Court exhausted every night. He worked himself twice as hard as any of his laborers. It seemed that no detail was too small for his attention.

Most nights he came to her bed, sometimes to make love to her; other nights he fell into an exhausted sleep, seemingly content to hold her. His presence was a source of comfort and confusion, for Felicity found it hard to reconcile the man who came to her in the nighttime with the cold and reserved stranger that Kilgarvan appeared to be during the day. It was as if the Earl of Kilgarvan was a mask that he donned, and only at night, in the privacy of their chambers, did he let the mask slip.

Felicity's own days were filled to overflowing. Each morning she spent an hour with Mr. Hamilton, who was teaching her the Gaelic tongue. The rest of her day was spent training the new servants and supervising the renovations. Under her management, Arlyn Court began to lose its air of musty abandonment. Rooms were freshly painted, and she browsed through pattern books to select wallpapers. Drapes were replaced, carpets cleaned, every stick of furniture polished within an inch of its life.

Copper pots and pans of every size were ordered for the kitchen, and the meals were served on delicate china dishes, accompanied by newly ordered silver plate. Perhaps inspired by her newly stocked kitchen, Nora Murphy now sent up meals that were greatly improved in their variety. Or perhaps it was not so much the new utensils as it was the threat of dismissal that had prompted the change in her attitude.

But for all the notice he took of the improvements, Kilgarvan might as well have been living in a shack and dining on bacon and potatoes. It irked her that he took for granted all the work she was doing to restore their home.

She wondered how it came to be that a man who was so courteous and kind to all others could be so neglectful and indifferent toward his wife.

Seventeen

They existed in an uneasy truce, each knowing that the situation could not last, and yet also not wanting to be the first to break the truce. The state of affairs was far too fragile to last. The end, when it came, was as sudden as it was expected.

Felicity was feeling quite pleased with herself. Just this morning she had taken the opportunity to practice her Gaelic on Nora Murphy. The cook, who had greeted Felicity's intrusion into the kitchen with her customary scowl, beamed with delight upon being addressed in her native tongue. She had launched into a torrent of words, almost too fast for Felicity to follow. But Felicity understood enough to know that the cook was praising the kindness and learning of her new mistress.

In the end it had been all that Felicity could do to make her escape.

She left the kitchen and climbed the stairs that led to the public rooms. As she approached the room that Kilgarvan used as his estate office, the door swung open, and her husband's figure appeared.

"May I have a word with you?" he asked.

"Of course."

At his gesture she stepped into his office, and he

followed. The estate office was a small room, whose double windows overlooked the stableyard. On the opposite wall, rows of shelves held account books, ledgers, seed catalogs, auction notices and such. On the desk was a small pile of letters, next to which was a pen and inkwell and a sheaf of blank paper. Apparently Kilgarvan had been doing his correspondence when he heard her steps.

There was a battered but serviceable chair with padded armrests behind the desk, and on the other side two armless straight-backed chairs no doubt intended for servants or tradesmen.

"Please sit down," he said, moving behind the desk.

"If it will be but a moment, then I will stand," Felicity said with a trace of unease. She had no intention of sitting opposite Kilgarvan, as if she were a mere petitioner and not his wife.

Kilgarvan shrugged his shoulders. He did not sit down, but rather picked up a letter from the desk.

"I wished to inform you that we will be having a guest," he said.

"Is it someone I know? Your mother perhaps?"

"No, Lady Kilgarvan remains in Dublin, although she sends her kind regards to us both," he replied. "No, the visitor is a Mr. Hobson, with whom I wish to consult on a matter of business."

"I see." She paused for a moment, wondering how on earth he expected her to house and entertain a guest. Her renovations were in that in-between stage where everything was well begun, but yet nothing was near completion. She could hardly assign a guest to a room that was half-painted, or worse yet, where the old paper had been stripped off, and new paper not yet arrived.

She tapped one finger against her cheek as she thought. "I suppose the north guest room could be made ready. The water-damaged floorboards were repaired, and the plasterers finished last week. And I think, although I am not certain, that it was on the list to be painted this week. So as long as your Mr. Hobson does not mind the smell of fresh paint, I think we could be ready for him."

"I am certain he will have no objection," Kilgarvan said. "According to his letter he should be here within four or five days."

Four or five days? That meant that Mr. Hobson was already on his way, no doubt in response to an invitation issued by her husband. Strange that it had not occurred to Kilgarvan to warn her sooner that she needed to prepare for guests. Was it because he had faith in her ability to organize the house? Or had it simply been a gentlemanly oversight, his not realizing that his wife might not find it convenient to entertain strangers while in the midst of renovations?

"We will be ready for his arrival. But, pray tell, what business does Mr. Hobson wish to discuss?"

Kilgarvan shifted on his feet. "Mr. Hobson owns several factories in the north of Ireland. He has written me about the possibility of starting a factory to manufacture linen here in Glenmore."

"A factory?" Glenmore seemed an odd location for such a venture. It seemed to her that a factory was better suited to a more populous location, one with ready access to markets and suppliers.

"Yes, a factory. In Glenmore," Kilgarvan said, biting off each word. "Mr. Hobson will provide the knowledge and experience to start the venture, and I—that is, we—will provide the capital."

A factory seemed an odd concept in such a rural setting. And yet, if such a thing could be made to work, it would be a very good thing for all concerned. Kilgarvan would have the advantage of a good investment, and it would add jobs for his people that were not subject to the vagaries of agriculture.

"But what of this Mr. Hobson? He is experienced, but what kind of experience does he have? Are his factories profitable? Are his workers treated fairly? One hears such dreadful stories of the conditions in some of these factories, where the workers are treated little better than slaves."

Her words were intended as an innocent question, but her husband exploded as if she had insulted him. "I do not need you to tell me how to manage my affairs," Kilgarvan said. "What do you know of Ireland, or Kilgarvan, or of what my people need? And yet you hold your money over my head as a weapon, insisting that I explain every decision to you."

His words sparked off her own anger. "How dare you speak to me in such a fashion, when I am simply trying to help you?"

"I do not want your help. I never wanted you here at all."

"You never wanted *me,*" she said. "You only wanted my money."

She stared him full in the face, daring him to contradict her. He stared back at her, stubborn, immovable. His eyes were dark, fathomless pools. She searched in vain for some trace of the man who was her husband, but Kilgarvan the friend had disappeared behind the mask that was the Earl of Kilgarvan.

The silence stretched between them as she waited

for him to deny her accusations. When she could
stand it no longer, she broke the silence. "So, the
truth at last," she said, her throat so tight that she
could barely swallow.

"Felicity—" he began, but she cut him off with an
upraised hand.

"Do not lie to me now," she said, suddenly weary.
"It is ill-becoming of you. We both know that the
Kilgarvan land is your true love, and marrying me
was simply a means of securing what you prized most.
And I am too weary to argue with you anymore. Your
obstinate pride will be the undoing of you, but I will
not stay to see it happen. You can have the money; I
give it to you freely. And I will leave you here with
the money and your land. I am sure you will be very
happy together."

With that, she spun on her heel and left the room.
As she walked away, a part of her listened, hoping to
hear him calling her back. Hoping to hear him say
that she was wrong, and that he wanted her to be
part of his life. But there was only silence.

The next morning she stood in the front hall,
watching as a servant loaded the last of her baggage
into a pony cart, and then began covering it with an
oilcloth. The skies, which had been a dull, leaden
gray all morning, took this as a signal, and a soft rain
began to fall.

Felicity pulled on her gloves and adjusted her
cloak. She wondered what was keeping Dennis
O'Connor. He should have been here by now.

"It is a miserable day for travel," Kilgarvan said
from somewhere behind her.

She did not turn around. "We have seen worse,"

she said, addressing the air in front of her, remembering their journey from Cork. How long had it been since that torrential rainstorm, when they had been forced to seek shelter in Drisheen? Had it really been only two months ago? It seemed far longer. So much had happened since then. She had found her husband, and had lost him. Kilgarvan had chosen the land instead of her.

She could not stay here. Not when each day, each hour made her more miserable than the last. For it was all too clear that Kilgarvan did not want her here. He had determined from the start to shut her out of his life. And nothing she tried, whether gentle reason or stubborn argument, had served to put a dent in his convictions.

Perhaps things would have been different if they had made a better start to their marriage. If she had not insisted on trying to control Kilgarvan with her dowry. If Kilgarvan had not angered her by leaving her alone when she needed his support to face the London gossip.

There was blame enough to go around. For that matter, if only one of them had been sensible enough to insist on a more conventional period of engagement, they might have avoided this whole mess altogether.

Or they might not have. Their marriage might have been doomed from the start, simply because of her wealth and his poverty. Kilgarvan had enough pride for a dozen men, and he resented her for his misfortune.

And she had wounded his pride with her insistence on trying to help him, to be part of his life. The more she had tried to prove her worth to him, the more he had closed her out, until she could see no way to break the patterns of their behavior.

Just then Dennis O'Connor appeared on horseback. Behind him came a servant, leading Felicity's gray gelding and the pony that Bridget O'Connor was to use.

It was time. She took a deep breath, and then began to speak. "You will find a letter in my sitting room addressed to Mr. Clutterbuck. A shipment of furniture should be arriving from Cork City any day now. Mrs. O'Connor will know what is to be done with it. The renovators have their list of tasks, but you should assign someone to keep an eye on their progress."

Felicity turned, unable to deny herself one last glimpse of Kilgarvan. It was some relief to see that he looked as miserable as she felt. His eyes were bloodshot, and the lines on his face told of a sleepless night.

"But where will you be?"

"I have not decided. Paris, perhaps. Or Venice is lovely this time of year. But do not worry. There will be no scandal. And should you need to contact me for any reason, you may apply to Lord Rutland for my direction."

Kilgarvan stretched out one hand as if to touch her, and then the arm fell back to his side. "Felicity, you do not have to leave," he said.

She shook her head. "Yes, I do," she insisted. "You truly do not wish me to stay—you merely feel guilty at having banished me."

She had to leave. For her own sanity. Staying would only torment her with images of what she could not have. The only cure for her ache was time and distance.

* * *

Dennis O'Connor and his sister Bridget were her companions for the two-day journey to Nedeen. There she bade them farewell, and boarded a ship bound for Cork. The Cork harbor was filled with ships, and she could have had her choice of a dozen different vessels to carry her to England or to the Continent. But she had no wish to return to England, to face the inevitable questions about her marriage. Nor did she wish to resume the life of an aimless wanderer.

Instead she took passage for Dublin. Upon her arrival she met with their agent, Mr. Perry, and instructed him to find her a suitable residence.

Then she sent a card to Lady Kilgarvan, informing the dowager that she was in town.

Lady Kilgarvan called at her hotel the very next day.

They exchanged pleasantries, and Felicity assured Lady Kilgarvan that her son was well and that he sent his kind regards to her.

"And how did you find Kilgarvan? Was it as you expected?"

"Yes and no," Felicity said cautiously. "The countryside is very beautiful—"

"And the people are very poor," Lady Kilgarvan added.

"Indeed. But your son is hoping to change that, in time." Restoring his estates was all he lived for. It consumed his thoughts, and his heart, to the exclusion of all else.

"And you? Is this trip to Dublin a mere visit? From your letters I was under the impression that you planned to make Kilgarvan your home."

And so had she. "Circumstances changed," Felicity said.

"Did you leave by choice? Or because my son ill-treated you?"

She shook her head. "No, it was not that. But rather the improvements on the estate consumed his every waking hour. There seemed no reason for me to be there, so I left."

"I had hoped for better, but it seems he is just like his father," the countess said, shaking her head sadly. "Ours was a love match, and for the first few years life was wonderful. We came to Dublin for the Season and spent the rest of the year on the estate. But gradually the estate consumed more and more of my husband's time and attention. He had little energy to spare for anything else. Not for me, not for his son. It became an obsession with him. I began to spend more and more time in Dublin, and then one year I simply did not return. I don't think he noticed my absence at all."

"I doubt Kilgarvan will notice my absence either," Felicity said.

"But you love him." It was not quite a question.

"Yes." Felicity sighed, wondering at the impulse that made her share her feelings with the countess, when she had not even told Kilgarvan. "I left because I love him, and because I could not bear to stay there, knowing that I was his second choice."

She had lost her husband not to another woman, but to a dream of his birthright, and his love for his land. How could she possibly compete with a love that was part of his very soul? She had nothing to offer him except herself and the simple human warmth of her love. And that had not been enough for him.

"There, there," the countess said, moving to sit on the sofa, and patting Felicity's hand as if to comfort her. "All may not be lost. My son is still young. He may yet come to his senses."

Felicity forced herself to smile. "You may be right," she said, but for her own part she held no such hope.

Eighteen

It did not take Kilgarvan long to realize that his people blamed him for Felicity's departure. He could see it in their eyes as he visited the work sites in the valley, in the subdued greetings he received whenever he ventured into the village of Glenmore. Everywhere he went, the people inquired about the missing countess, and when Felicity was likely to return. He replied to their inquiries brusquely, not willing to admit that he did not know the answer to their questions. How could he tell them that he did not even know where his wife had gone?

Dennis O'Connor had escorted Felicity to Nedeen, from whence she had taken a ship to Cork City. From Cork she could have traveled to anywhere: Dublin, London, the Continent; for all he knew she was on a ship now, bound for some exotic land. He wondered if she were well, and if her thoughts turned to him as often as his turned in her direction.

At Arlyn Court it was worse. The servants gave him sidelong glances, their faces stiff with disapproval. Their loyalty to their mistress was only to be expected, since they owed their employment to Felicity. It was she who had chosen them, and her dowry that was paying their wages.

But even those who had known him the longest had turned against him. When he asked Mrs. O'Connor to ensure that the guest room was made ready for Mr. Hobson, she responded by lamenting Felicity's absence. According to his housekeeper, Felicity was a paragon of generosity, goodness and organization, and without its mistress Arlyn Court was liable to collapse.

Felicity had even managed to charm the irascible Nora Murphy, for Kilgarvan found himself receiving cold dinners of burned meat and undercooked potatoes, as the cook made plain her displeasure with her master.

It was not fair. Felicity had been here only two months. He had lived here all his life. Arlyn Court belonged to him; the Kilgarvan land was his birthright. His people should have chosen his side in any quarrel, and yet somehow his English wife had won their hearts.

It was impossible that her absence could make such a difference. And yet, as the days passed and there was no word from Felicity, he found himself spending less and less time at Arlyn Court. For the house where he had spent his life now seemed strangely empty.

And there were reminders of Felicity everywhere. Each room bore the imprint of her presence. Arlyn Court shone with grandeur as it had not for a dozen years. But it was a grandeur that excluded him. He was not part of this. He could never be.

He had expected that Felicity's departure would bring relief, an end to the impossible strain. No more would he have to justify every decision to her, and to beg his wife for money. No more would he be forced to endure the condemnation in her eyes as she saw the plight of his people. Without her constant questioning, he would be free of the doubts that plagued him, as he wondered if he was truly capable of restoring the estates.

But Felicity's absence brought no relief, no comfort. Nor even did the knowledge that she had repudiated the marriage contracts, instructing the solicitor to release whatever funds her husband required without her approval. It was what he had wanted all along, and yet the victory was hollow. The feeling of triumph was overshadowed by the memory of sorrow that he had brought to Felicity, and the sadness in her face as she had left him.

He had won the victory he sought, but he was haunted by the growing sense that he might have thrown away a far greater prize.

Late Friday evening, Mr. Hobson finally arrived. Kilgarvan had been looking forward to this visit as a welcome distraction, to keep him from brooding over Felicity's absence.

Seeing Mr. Hobson's fatigue, however, Kilgarvan had merely bidden him welcome, and seen that his guest was shown to a chamber and that a meal was sent up on a tray. He had invited Mr. Hobson to join him for breakfast the next morning, and it was at that meal that he first heard Mr. Hobson's ideas.

"I don't mind telling you, my lord, that the journey here would have taxed the strength of a young man. I see now why they call this the uncivilized part of Ireland. Why, the roads here are scarce fit for donkeys."

Mr. Hobson was a middle-aged man with thinning brown hair combed carefully over a shiny bald pate. He had a round face, and was full of smiles and hearty laughter, which gave the impression of affability and good humor. It was only when one looked closely that one saw that his smile never quite reached his eyes, which were dark and knowing, and seemed to miss no detail of his surroundings.

"I appreciate your making the journey," Kilgarvan said. "And as for the roads, I have laborers working even now to repair them."

Mr. Hobson nodded. "Yes, I saw them, though if they made any progress I could not see it. If I were you, I would hire an English supervisor to make sure the workers do not slack off. The Irish are not used to hard labor, but with enough supervision even the laziest of peasants can be made to turn in an honest day's work."

Kilgarvan eyed his guest, but there was no sign that Mr. Hobson was jesting.

"My workers have never given me cause for complaint," Kilgarvan said mildly.

"Of course, of course," Mr. Hobson agreed, seeming to realize that he had said too much. "But there is no harm in being firm. It is hardly the work they are used to."

Mr. Hobson carefully cut a piece of bacon, then speared it with a fork and lifted it to his mouth. He chewed the meat with careful deliberation, then swallowed.

Fortunately Nora Murphy's grudge against her employer did not extend to his guest. This morning's breakfast was a meal worthy of Felicity's tenure. But Mr. Hobson showed neither enjoyment of or displeasure with his food. He ate with mechanical precision, as if eating was simply an act that needed to be done, rather than a source of enjoyment.

Kilgarvan found it difficult to reconcile the image

of the man sitting before him with the shrewd businessman he was reported to be. Mr. Hobson had started life as a clerk in a factory in Belfast, rising rapidly to the position of manager, and then managed to raise enough capital to buy out the original owner. Within five years his factory had doubled in size; within ten he had added a glassworks, a spinning mill and an ironworks to his growing empire. He now owned shares in a dozen other factories and enterprises in the north.

Looking to expand his commercial empire to the south of Ireland, Mr. Hobson had journeyed to Cork, surveying possible sites for a new ironworks. Learning of his presence, Kilgarvan had written to Mr. Hobson, inviting him to visit to discuss a business proposition. Mr. Hobson's business sense had come highly recommended, but that did not make the man any easier to like.

It was not necessary that he like Mr. Hobson, Kilgarvan reminded himself. It was simply necessary that he be able to work with the man. After all, he knew his limitations. Any factory he started would need an experienced manager, and who better to consult than a man who had already started a dozen successful enterprises?

"So what is it you wished to speak with me about?" Mr. Hobson said, laying down his napkin beside his plate and pushing back his chair. "You hardly asked me here to discuss the state of your roads."

Kilgarvan took a sip of his tea and then set the cup down. "Mr. Hobson, I have heard that there is no one in Ireland who knows more about starting factories than you."

"That is very kind, my lord. I will say I have had my successes."

"I have a mind to start a linen factory here in Kilgarvan. As it is, my tenants and I are entirely too dependent on agriculture. I am looking for a partner to join me in this new venture."

"And your share would be the land? Or would you be furnishing the capital as well?" Mr. Hobson asked, coming straight to the point.

"Both," Kilgarvan said firmly. "But I have no experience in factories, and this is why I am seeking a partner."

Mr. Hobson stroked his chin. "Hmm. I would want to see the proposed site, and discuss your plans with you and your agent. I had not considered investing in Kerry, but there are possibilities here—yes, indeed, there are."

It was better than he had hoped for. He knew Mr. Hobson was too shrewd a businessman to commit himself wholly to such a scheme at once. Instead he would carefully consider all the angles. But even if Mr. Hobson did not agree to be his partner, at the very least Kilgarvan would have the benefit of his advice on the project.

After breakfast they went down to the village, and Kilgarvan showed Mr. Hobson the site he had chosen for the factory. The cascades from the lake-fed stream would provide more than sufficient energy for turning a mill wheel, and the stream itself would provide a constant supply of fresh water for the factory.

They returned to Arlyn Court and met with Dennis O'Connor in the estate office to review Kilgarvan's own plans. Mr. Hobson questioned everything, from the number of residents of the valley who could be hired as workers, to the amount of money that Kilgarvan was prepared to invest, and how long the earl was prepared to wait until the factory began turning a profit.

At last Mr. Hobson declared himself satisfied. "I was doubtful this morning, my lord," he said. "Others have tried to establish linen in the south, with no success. But your situation here is a very good one. You have the site and the capital, and the climate here will work in your favor. And although Kilgarvan is far from a city, once the road is rebuilt this will be no great inconvenience. In fact, it may be in your favor, for there is no need to pay your workers the wages they would expect in the city. From what I saw they will be grateful for any employment, and you can pay them half of what I must pay my own workers in Belfast."

"I intend to pay my workers fair wages," Kilgarvan said.

"Of course, but there is fair and then there is fair," Mr. Hobson replied. "It is not as if they are accustomed to the work, as Englishmen would be. We will need to hire experienced men to act as overseers, men who can read and write and follow directions."

There was truth in what Mr. Hobson said. Country folk did not expect city wages, nor could Kilgarvan expect his own farmers to easily turn their hands to factory work. Yet there was something in the way that Mr. Hobson expressed his ideas that set his back up.

Dennis O'Connor seemed to share his distaste. "I suppose you see it as good fortune that the Irish have so many children," he said softly. "For children can be employed in the factories, and paid even less than a grown man."

Mr. Hobson beamed approvingly at the agent, not realizing that Dennis was being ironic. "Another point in our favor, I must agree," he said. "And unlike their parents, the children can be taught English, and brought up to understand the modern way of doing things."

Kilgarvan's flesh crawled.

Dennis O'Connor's face darkened, and his right hand clenched into a fist.

"This has been a most . . . informative . . . discussion," Kilgarvan said, catching Dennis's eye and giving him a stern glare. "But I have taken up a great deal of your time, and I would be remiss if I did not offer you a chance to rest, while I attend to other business."

"Of course," Mr. Hobson said, his brow wrinkling in apparent puzzlement as he looked from Kilgarvan to Dennis, and then back to the earl. "I trust you will give my proposal all due consideration?"

"I will give your proposal the full consideration it deserves," Kilgarvan said firmly. "I will see you at dinner? We keep country hours here, and will dine at six."

"I look forward to it," Mr. Hobson said, rising from his chair. Then, with a short bow, he left the room.

Dennis held his silence until Mr. Hobson's footsteps could be heard ascending the main staircase. Then he firmly closed the door to the office and turned to face his friend.

"Gerald," he said, "tell me that you have not lost your wits. Tell me that you are not seriously considering a partnership with that arrogant bastard."

Kilgarvan shook his head. "I would not trust that man to run a stall at the fair, let alone with the welfare of our people."

The tension left Dennis's frame. "Good," he said. "I did not think so, but you have been acting so strangely since you returned . . ."

Dennis's words stung, but it hurt more to realize that his oldest friend had not been sure of his reaction. Dennis had actually thought him capable of a partnership with the odious Mr. Hobson.

"Have I really been so much of an ass?"

Dennis leaned back in his chair and crossed his legs. "Aye," he said. "Sure and we know you have a good heart under it all. But ever since you have come back from England, you seem to be trying to make Kilgarvan over into an English village. It is no sin to be poor, no sin to be Irish."

"I know that."

"Then why wouldn't you teach Felicity Gaelic?"

"Because it was better that the servants learned English."

"Did it ever occur to you that they might not want to learn English? That they are proud of who they are?"

Of course his people were proud of their Irish heritage. It was a pride he shared. But such pride was no excuse for ignorance and superstition that kept them mired in poverty.

"Are you saying I was wrong to build the fishing weir? To plan the new village? To try to bring the factory in, to give our people a chance at a new life?"

"No, no, I am not saying that. The weir, the houses, those are all good things. And the new factory could be a good thing as well. You just need to think a bit, first. Maybe our people do not want a grand factory, if it means losing who they are. Maybe it would be better not to try to do so much at once. All I'm asking is that you think before you do anything that you will regret."

Felicity had tried to tell him as much, but he had not been willing to listen. He had been too blind, too certain that he, and he alone, knew best. How often had he raged to Felicity over the backwardness of his people? How often had he decried their ignorance, and declared that only by adopting English methods of industry and commerce could they hope to survive?

The encounter with Mr. Hobson had been like looking into a dark mirror, one that magnified all his own faults and misconceptions. It was a terrible glimpse into the future, and what he could become if he allowed his own compulsions to drive him.

It was a hard truth that Dennis had told him, but it was a truth that he was finally willing to hear.

"You are a good friend," Kilgarvan said. "I know I do not say so often enough."

"Ah, well, every man needs a friend who can knock sense into his stubborn head," Dennis said, trying to lighten the mood.

"Well, next time don't wait so long," Kilgarvan said.

"What are you going to do about Mr. Hobson? If it were up to me, I'd show him the door, and help him out with a boot to his backside."

It was a tempting thought, but hardly appropriate behavior. "I think not," Kilgarvan said. "He is my guest, after all, here at my invitation. I will simply send him on his way tomorrow. After I tell him that I have reconsidered my decision to partner with him."

"That's better than he deserves," Dennis said.

That would solve the problem of Mr. Hobson. But what was he to do about Felicity?

Nineteen

Felicity gazed out the drawing room window at the busy Dublin street scene revealed below. But her mind was not on the bustle of the street, but rather on the countryside that she had left behind. The endless golden summer had finally drawn to a close, and autumn had arrived. And with it would come harvesttime. Every hand at Kilgarvan would be turned to the task of bringing in the crops before the first frost.

And Lord Kilgarvan was certain to be in the thick of it. Such an important event would require his every moment of supervision. She could almost picture him, his cravat undone, his dark hair tousled by the wind as he strode the fields, encouraging his tenants as they labored. And if the weather held, and the harvest was a good one, afterward there would be the traditional harvest ball for the tenants.

She felt a pang of sadness. She missed Arlyn Court and Kilgarvan's valley. She missed the country folk, who had set aside their pride to welcome their new countess, despite her English birth. Kilgarvan had crept into her mind and heart in a way that no other place ever had.

Or perhaps it was not Kilgarvan the land, but Kil-

garvan the gentleman that her heart was pining for.
Not Kilgarvan as he had been, cold and driven by his
responsibilities. But the man she had seen glimpses
of, the man who could be a lover and a friend.

The man she had fallen in love with. It was ironic,
for her love was the reason she had left him. If she
had felt mere affection, then she could have stayed
at Arlyn Court—stayed to make the county her home.
After all, all she had ever wanted was a place to set
down roots, and a husband who respected her and
treated her affectionately.

But Kilgarvan had shown her that she could have
so much more: a husband who was both friend and
lover. And yet any chance for happiness had been
doomed from the start, ever since she had insisted
upon that ridiculous marriage settlement. His pride
and her stubbornness had combined to send them
down a path from which there was no turning back.

"He would come if you told him, my dear," Lady
Kilgarvan observed.

Felicity turned her unseeing gaze from the street
scene, toward her mother-in-law. The dowager countess sat in a chair next to the fireplace, her attention
seemingly fixed upon her embroidery frame.

"I beg your pardon?" Felicity said. "Who would
come, and what would I tell him?"

"My son may be a fool," Lady Kilgarvan said, continuing to set perfectly even stitches. "But if you were
to tell him that you are with child, he would come
for you."

"How did you know?" Felicity asked, too shocked
to dissemble. She had told no one. It had been only
a fortnight since the physician had confirmed Felicity's growing suspicions.

Lady Kilgarvan smiled. "Don't worry. It does not

show yet, unless someone knows you very well indeed." She paused, tying a knot in the thread and then cutting it off with a small pair of scissors. Reaching over into the work basket on the table next to her, she rooted around until she found the skein of yarn that she was looking for.

"May I ask when the child will be born?"

"The physician was not sure. Late April or perhaps May," she replied. Although the physician was unwilling to commit himself, in her heart Felicity was certain that this child had been conceived on the night of Nora Connolly's wedding.

"And how long are you planning on waiting before you tell your husband?"

"That is my decision to make," Felicity said.

"Of course. But he will have to learn sometime. You will not be able to hide your condition for much longer in society. Better that he hear it from you than from an acquaintance."

The dowager countess had a good point, but Felicity did not want to hear it. She knew that Kilgarvan would come as soon as he heard the news. But she did not want him to come merely because he felt it was his obligation. She did not want to see him, knowing that his care was for the child she bore, and not for herself.

And yet what else could she do? She could not hide away forever. Eventually she would be forced to confront him.

"I will consider what you say," Felicity said. "But pray tell me, what do you think of Lady Kinsale's invitation to visit her estate? Would you like to leave Dublin for a bit?"

She was relieved when the dowager accepted the change of topic with good grace. Felicity counted herself lucky that the dowager had consented to leave her sister and brother-in-law, and to join Felicity in the Dublin town house she had rented. The dowager had proven a good companion, although sometimes she saw more than Felicity was willing to reveal.

Felicity's arrival had coincided with the start of the Little Season, and Lady Kilgarvan's presence had helped establish her in Dublin society. A few greeted her coolly, but the tight-knit community seemed to find nothing unusual in Felicity's presence. Indeed it seemed expected that a woman of Felicity's rank and breeding would prefer the company of genteel society to an estate in the Irish hinterland.

Although she had relinquished control of the bulk of her fortune to Kilgarvan, she continued to draw upon the generous allowance that she had been allotted. It was more than sufficient for her and Lady Kilgarvan's needs. In what seemed no time at all she had leased a fashionable town house, complete with servants and a cook trained in France. Soon she had settled into the life of a Dublin aristocrat.

It was not what she had wanted or hoped for. But it was what she had, and she was determined to make the most of it.

Kilgarvan patted his breast pocket, making certain that the letter from Felicity was still inside. A foolish gesture, he knew, but he clung to the letter as a tangible sign that all was not yet hopeless.

For Felicity had not gone to France, nor Italy, nor even to England. Instead she had written him from Dublin. She could have put herself beyond his reach, but instead she had chosen to reside in Dublin. In

the company of his mother, no less. It gave him hope
that there was still time to put things right.

He arrived in Dublin in the late afternoon, and
went directly to see her.

He rapped the brass door knocker hard enough to
be heard in the next county. After a moment the door
swung open, revealing a footman.

"Yes?" the footman prompted with a faint sneer.

Kilgarvan was suddenly conscious of how he must
look, fresh from the road with the dust on him, and
his clothes wrinkled. No wonder the footman
thought him a disreputable character. Perhaps he
should have stopped first at a hotel, to change his
attire and wash up. But he had been too impatient
to stop, too anxious to arrive.

"Is your mistress at home?"

"Yes, but—"

He did not need to hear any more. Kilgarvan
stepped over the threshold, brushing aside the slightly
built footman. "I am Lord Kilgarvan," he said frostily.

The servant stared at him, gape-mouthed. Kilgarvan doffed his hat and handed it to the footman, who
accepted it and closed his mouth with an audible
click. Then he removed his coat and handed that to
the footman as well.

The sounds of feminine laughter drifted down hall.
He then realized that Felicity had guests, but having
come so far he was not willing to be turned away.

He left the footman behind him and ventured
down the hall. The sounds of conversation grew
stronger, and then through an open door on the left,
he glimpsed a salon.

As he stepped into the salon, the women's voices
hushed, and he found himself the focus of a dozen
pairs of eyes.

He recognized only two of the women present: his mother, who looked pleased to see him, and his wife, who did not.

Felicity appeared every inch the elegant woman he had met in London. Her amber silk gown was of the first stare of fashion, as was her elaborately styled coiffure. Her expression was carefully neutral, giving little hint of her feelings.

"I beg your pardon, ladies," he said with a short bow. "But I must speak with my wife. Felicity, if you would be so kind?"

The ladies began to whisper among themselves as his identity was revealed, but he had eyes only for Felicity. She looked at him, then back at her guests. At last she seemed to make up her mind.

"Ladies, if you will excuse me for a moment," she said, rising from her chair. "And, Mother, if you would pour?"

"Of course," his mother said.

Kilgarvan waited as Felicity threaded her way among the chairs.

She offered no word of greeting, no inquiries after his health or the difficulties of the journey. He followed her down the hall, noting her anger in the stiff set of her back, and the way her head was held unnaturally high.

She led him to a library at the end of the hall.

"Why have you come?"

He had imagined this moment a thousand times. But now that he was here with her, so close he could touch her, all of his carefully rehearsed speeches flew out of his head.

"I came to fetch you back to Kilgarvan. Where you belong."

Her eyes were wary. "Kilgarvan is your home, not mine. You made that abundantly clear to me."

He winced at the pain in her voice. He reached out a hand to touch her, but she stepped back, out of reach. "I can think of no reason to return," she said.

"Because I need you. Kilgarvan needs you," he said.

"You have the money. That is all you wanted. Any housekeeper could take my place at Kilgarvan." She turned, and he felt desperation as he realized she could walk out of his life forever.

"Then come with me because I love you. Because I am lost without you."

She turned back toward him, hope warring with disbelief plain to read in her face.

"If you loved me, then why did you let me leave?"

"Because I was a fool," he said honestly. "Because I could not see past my pride and my fears. I was afraid that I was not worthy of my responsibilities, afraid that I could not cope with the burden of the estate. I was afraid of becoming just like my father, whose plans had ruined the estate instead of saving it."

He took a deep breath, his head bent down. "And there you were, everything that I was not: sophisticated, cultured, far more knowledgeable than I in the ways of managing great wealth. Every time I looked at you, I felt I did not measure up in your eyes."

"But I never said that. I never even thought that," Felicity said. "All I wanted to do was help."

"I know now. It was my own self-doubts that poisoned the atmosphere. I could not bear the rejection I read in your eyes, so I pushed you farther and farther away, until in the end I forced you to leave. I know I must have hurt you terribly."

"I thought you did not care," Felicity said. "I thought you had no feelings for me."

He shook his head slowly, then reached out and took her hands in his. "No, it was that I was blind. I did not know what I had lost until you were gone. Arlyn Court is empty without you. I cannot exist like this. Please tell me that it is not too late to put things right."

Felicity felt her heart swell with emotion. There was a burning hope in Kilgarvan's eyes that matched the rising hope within her own breast.

"What of the harvest?" she asked.

He blinked, nonplussed. "The harvest? I imagine they've started it by now. But why do you ask?"

He had left Kilgarvan at harvesttime to come to her. He could have waited, but instead he had placed his need for her ahead of his responsibility to the land.

"I have my own share of stubbornness and pride," Felicity warned him.

He gave her hand a gentle squeeze. "And you know all the worst of my faults," he said. "But I promise you, if you come back with me to Kilgarvan, I will prove to you that you are loved and cherished."

Cherished. She liked the sound of that word.

"And I promise to love you in return," she said. "And I will come with you to Kilgarvan, for I think our son should be born among his people."

It took a moment for her words to sink in.

"Son?"

"Or daughter," she affirmed. "In the spring, if all is well."

Kilgarvan laughed, wrapping his arms around her in a fierce hug, then covering her face with kisses.

"You don't know how happy you have made me," he said. "I just hope my son doesn't inherit my faults."

"Take me home," she said.

ABOUT THE AUTHOR

Patricia Bray is the author of three Zebra Regency romances: *A London Season, An Unlikely Alliance,* and *Lord Freddie's First Love.* She loves to hear from her readers, and you may write to her at P.O. Box 273, Endicott, NY 13761. Please enclose an SASE if you wish a reply.

**LOVE STORIES YOU'LL NEVER FORGET . . .
IN ONE FABULOUSLY ROMANTIC NEW LINE**

BALLAD ROMANCES

Each month, four new historical series by both beloved and brand-new authors will begin or continue. These linked stories will introduce proud families, reveal ancient promises, and take us down the path to true love. In Ballad, the romance doesn't end with just one book . . .

COMING IN JULY
EVERYWHERE BOOKS ARE SOLD

The Wishing Well Trilogy:
CATHERINE'S WISH, by Joy Reed.
When a woman looks into the wishing well at Honeywell House, she sees the face of the man she will marry.

Titled Texans:
NOBILITY RANCH, by Cynthia Sterling
The three sons of an English earl come to Texas in the 1880s to find their fortunes . . . and lose their hearts.

Irish Blessing:
REILLY'S LAW, by Elizabeth Keys
For an Irish family of shipbuilders, an ancient gift allows them to "see" their perfect mate.

The Acadians:
EMILIE, by Cherie Claire
The daughters of an Acadian exile struggle for new lives in 18th-century Louisiana.